AF364137

To all those who believed in this once-wretched child —
I am forever indebted to your kindness...

Preface: Ramblings, murmurs, and tales of long-lost events and future occurrences.

Evening! Come, sit by the fire. Warm yourself. Help yourself to a hot beverage or two. This book can—and should—be enjoyed at your own leisure, pace, and order. There is no set beginning, and no end, but when you open and close it; the book is yours to do with as you see fit.

Throughout this compilation, you will find stories narrated in the first person — these are indicated with a campfire icon. Think of them less as short stories and more as prose poetry, chronicled in the style of an old bardic storyteller sitting beside you by the fire.

There is prophecy to be found in understanding human nature, for if history repeats itself, so too shall human reasoning. Enjoy!

What Awaits You

Your Spiders Within

Once upon a bluer sky, in times of chateaus and widowed blades, I was nothing but a vagabond. Travel was my prayer, the roadside and green brush my stately manor, and the path my church. As was common for the trade, I would become acquainted with countless others: some, priests of pauperism like myself; others, who knelt at the altar of gold; and others still, who did neither.

It is from those trying and tumultuous—yet magical—times that I bring you naught but a cautionary tale, wrapped in bards' robes, retold for your entertainment. For it so happens that, through my travels in that courtly age, I found myself the most strange and otherworldly of friendships — a group of Spiders!

Now, it might seem rather radical, but I assure you, it is no exaggeration. They were, indeed, spiders — eight legs and all. And, just as most would tend to steer clear of such companionship, I found my sentiments quite opposed. I was intrigued, completely drawn in by their peculiarly *weighted* view on matters of life. Although the circumstances of our meeting are not important to this tale, my subsequent adventure with these furry prickly predators is.

Five of them there were: two were young, no more than children but visibly arachnoid; three were adults, lithe and large — yet, to the human eye, seemingly no different to the ordinary peasantry so common at the time. It is through this more socially pleasant humanoid form that magnificent conversations began to take hold of our daily meetings; nothing more than small talk at first, but as I grew accustomed to their true spindly shape, our talks delved into all manner of topics, from the philosophical to the nonsensical. "So is the world!" they would exclaim between hoarse bursts of chittering laughter.

In one of those conversations lies the start of all of my problems — for, in my naïveté, I suggested that we six, due to our newfound camaraderie, should travel together, to form a new connection with the natural path ahead of all.

And so they did — packed up their webbed possessions and followed me through the earthen and the thorny thicket. But I was a fool—well-meaning, but a right fool nonetheless—for one never truly considers the difficulty of sharing a homestead with spiders. As well-mannered as my friends were, their natural disposition and arachnoid urges were not welcome roadside companions.

There I was, melting contentedly into a cup of warm, freshly-boiled tea, the sweet, leathery black aroma caressing my nostrils like a morning lover, when a large clump of white strands fell all around me and into my pot — *webs*. Thick, sticky, white spider webs. Now, I believe myself to be a patient and understanding man, but when the incident repeated itself ad nauseam, ruining not only breakfast, but midday stew and supper picnic, I knew I would not be able to take much more.

A confrontation was inevitable. One morning, as they were lazily swinging and swooping from their treetop beds, I brought up the issue. Back then I was a hot-headed youth, though, short-fused and quick-tempered — although, can I truly be blamed for raising my voice? Many an innocent teapot had already fallen victim to their incessant fibrous maiming. My sage water being ruined, I could handle... but when the third batch of quality barley tea—which had necessitated a machiavellian appraisal scheme just to acquire—was ruined, well... I lost it.

It was that moment, however, that I discovered what should have been quite an obvious truth: spiders rather dislike being screamed at.

I ran, ran faster than I thought my weary legs could manage, through bush and field, over stream and under stone bridge. Their chattering mouthparts were never too far behind, twin fangs clashing and stinging in anticipation of the gooey insides soon to flood them. At one moment—when the hair at the back of my neck could feel the sharp caress of their hunter's instinct, and my legs, ridden with cramps and internal pain, felt like waterlogged beams under a pier—I was graced with salvation.

A large, empty lake stood, imposing, in front of me, its sandy shores now going on forever in an endless downward slope. You would expect it to even out at some point, but it endlessly it dragged you down. A once-magnificent reservoir of life's ambrosia, now nothing but a hollow husk, a symbol of time's all-encompassing philosophy of death.

Yet herein lay my salvation, for as I blundered around in the sand, going deeper into the pit, I noticed that the center of the lake had a hole like a massive eye. Into the sky it peered, an eye within a toothless mouth, devouring sight and light alike and—before I knew it—devouring me. For I fell in, stumbling, reaching with my foot for that next sandy step but finding only air, and an ironic welcoming breeze as I plummeted down into the depths of the world.

The fall was long, yet fear made it longer still. A primeval abyss, with something truly ancient waiting at the bottom, as if every primal emotion had manifested into a palpable aura that flooded the senses. I readied myself for the impact, tensing all muscles and closing my eyes shut with such force that bright spots engulfed them, but it never came. Instead, a slimy, scaly limb of unspeakable size coiled around me, and the bright shaft of moonlight illuminated a straight beam into the depths, slowly revealing the gargantuan creature to whom the limb belonged.

First an elongated snout, then two house-sized nostrils, and finally the eyes: ichorous stars piercing through my very flesh, shining with heavenly fury and hellish grace, shunting my soul from my body, and finally its voice. When it spoke, the fetid smell of a thousand rotting corpses invaded my nose and made me retch; yet, far underneath, I could sense a more pleasant aroma, perhaps the fragrance of a forgotten memory, lingering yet in the soul's past. Its voice boomed—deafening, threatening, a hurricane whisper—and a pause preceded each word, as if struggling. Its forked tongue flicking like a massive banner, so the great serpent spoke:

O'er tree, shore, stone, I am
Stretched thinly still, my bloated heart
For this, prayer, golden gramme
Violet-bleached soul, will fall apart

I was stunned, stuck pondering the words of this colossal reptile — was he describing himself? Or was he pretending to be someone... me, perhaps? Suddenly, the carriage of my thoughts was shunted from the road by sounds resonating from the entrance. The spiders had fallen in.

The two children, eight-legged in their nature, easily grabbed on and used instinctual webbing to stave off falling, but their parents, now more man than arachnid, plummeted. I observed, awestruck, as the three gained speed and flailed around, desperate. *Why didn't they change back into spiders?* Their airborne squirming was cut short as the snakelike beast opened its mouth, revealing two reddish, rusted fangs; as they fell into its pitlike mouth, its great jaws clamped shut like a great pearl of thunder.

It may be remiss of me, but I do not remember much of the event after that calamity... only waking up in an unknown clearing, two small spiders by my side, still in fruitful sleep. I pondered for many a night after: *Why, oh why, hadn't the three adults simply shifted and escaped? And why had I been spared?* For the latter I have no answer to give as of the writing of this tale, but for the former:

Beware the changing of your shape, for who knows the true form of your limbs, the eyes of your mind, but your childish self, awestruck, gazing upon you through the mirror of your soul?

Malina's Demon Named Lust

Malina was a special girl. All children are the stars in their parent's eyes, beautiful, brilliant spots that forever change and illuminate their lives, but Malina's light was never so distant or cold; her radiance was like the sun, warm and homely and all too human.

It is often said that darkness devours most sweetly that which shines the brightest, and it is a sad day indeed whenever shadow manages to snuff out one the few bright candles in this life. And so, ever since her conception, Malina was accosted by the dark, by that which maliciously hides at the corner of your vision — that which stares at you from behind every tree in a somber, mist-fallen forest.

Yet, despite all of this, her childhood was one of happiness and glee — years that, although occasionally twisted by natural, spontaneous instances of sadness, gilded her memory like a warm summer smile. It was not until her thirteenth birthday that this delightful ride through life would suddenly suffer a catastrophic crash, a turnaround so immediate, so unexpected, that it felt unfair. It was the day that it first appeared before her.

What was supposed to be a day of celebration, of singing and rejoicing surrounded by family and friends, had, since the moment she had woken up, been tainted by the somber, azure tone of fear, for she had experienced what every young girl her age fears — her first period, like a biological boogeyman, had decided to take away her innocence on that sacred day.

She had, of course, heard stories of the unwelcome changes prophesied by this crimson mark, the never-ending cycle of suffering and emotional instability that would now forever be part of her life; but she was Malina, and—like the sun—she had never been one to shy away, to reject change. But, standing there in her pajamas, staring unblinking at the sanguine spot now decorating the middle of her bed, she was consumed by fear.

She told her mother, of course. She hated lies and, even more, she hated lying to her mother, with her large blue eyes that seemed to glisten like aquamarine at the bottom of a calm river. So her mother had talked, and she had listened, but even after all had been said and done, with hugs lovingly exchanged, that knot in the pit of her chest remained ever tight.

And thus, like a secret, foul ingredient, fear had soured and spoiled the taste of all the day's activities; even the three-layer chocolate cake, her favorite, had felt bland and chewy; and, as the night grew closer and the guests slowly left the house, her appetite for fun dimmed. For the first time ever on any birthday night she longed for bedtime, for the solace and comfort that the blanket of dreams would provide.

No dreams, however, would soothe her soul that night. It was 11:30 P.M., far past her normal bedtime, when she finally retreated to her room. It was a small, hand-me-down cubical courtesy of her brother, decorated by a singular rectangular wooden bedframe and a couple of drawers on the frame's base, brought together by a dinky circular rug and a large double window. She liked her room; it was not pretty but practical, not eccentric, but why should it be? She *did* only sleep there.

Only after her parents had wished her good night, only after her mother had parted her hair and placed a sweet and soft kiss on her forehead, only after the lights had been turned off and the room fell into a deafening silence, did she—for the first time ever—hate her room.

Her silken green curtains, which always lifted her spirits in the morning, now draped over the incoming moonlight like funerary robes. Her bedframe, which had always given her comfort, now unsettled her — for it felt too close to the ground, too close to the edge of the room where the light barely graced. But these were merely droplets, individually small inconformities against a very large ocean of calm; what truly frightened her, what made her skin crawl and the hairs on the back of her neck stand on edge as if electrified, was that she was sure—impossibly so—that there was something in the corner of her room.

This is some sort of illusion, she thought, *there had been nothing there when the light had been turned off and no change had been observed since, so why, why was there now this shape?* Humanoid, somehow twisted, and why in *that* corner? The dark one, where even on the brightest of nights, only a sliver of moonlight managed to pierce the blackness.

Her terror only grew as her tear-infused eyes adapted to the penumbra of the room — this was no illusion, no trick of the light; she was staring at a human back. The being was extremely pale and malnourished, its vertebrae sticking out of its curved back like jagged, nightmarish spikes, its skin stretched tight over its bones and the very little muscle that accompanied them.

She could not make out its head, still bathed in gloom, but somehow she knew—she just knew—that *it knew* she was there. Its arms and legs remaining hidden, the creature stood incredibly still but for one small, yet rhythmic, movement — a heaving of its back, accompanied by a horrific gurgling sound, as if it had shredded its vocal cords with a razor and was now running foul, rancid air forcibly through them.

And so she cried; she cried all night, unable to close her eyes and drift away into unconsciousness, chained down by the oppressive thought that, if she so much as looked away for a second, her unwelcome nighttime visitor would turn around, and then...

Then... she did not know, and as far as she was concerned she did not want to know. She didn't have the heart to tell her parents that next day — what would they think, a girl of her age still fantasizing about unnatural monsters, still scared of the dark, of the deep? And so she waited with bated breath, waited and thought and was consumed by a genuine terror for the approaching dusk... but she was spared, for there was no visitor to be seen. As the days passed and her experience faded into memory, she began to naively believe that it had all been a bad dream, brought on by that first, world-shattering period.

It was only the next month, on the eve of that dreaded moment, where she would flow for a second time, and her corner would again be occupied by that monstrosity. This time she heard it first — that rasping, forceful breathing, rough and painful like nails on chalkboard, again and again reverberating around the room, ripping her out of her dream and shunting her back into that ever-real nightmare.

This time it was closer — it had to be, because most of its body was now in the direct path of the moonlight. Still it was turned around and—thankfully, she thought—still its head obscured by an impenetrable void.

Its arms were impossibly long, reaching down to its knees

and ending in four long, skeletal fingers; its fingernails, thin and sharp, were decorated with a deep rouge that looked like dried blood. Its legs were squalid unguligrade walking sticks, ending in hooves covered by matted and mangy gray fur, spots of the same dark liquid covering them as well.

A truly demonic tableau, populated by sudden spasms that shook its skeletal form as if shocked, making Malina feel as if it would pounce at any moment — at any moment, it could turn around and then... Still, she lay motionless, a grim tear down her pale cheek. At points where her fear crescendoed, where the terror would grip her very soul and squeeze so viciously that she begged for an end, a new instrument would join her orchestra of misery as the wheezing that she assumed was the creature's breath accelerated.

Like an old violin being played by a violent madman, the ragged and out-of-tune chords were violated by the bow such that they screeched and screamed as they jumped octaves. Her ears felt like they were bleeding — that was the sound it made when she was most afraid; that, as she would come to know so well, was the sound of its laughter.

And so, the cyclical nature of her suffering was revealed — every month, her period would come, and every month her ma-niacal accoster would show itself, ever closer, its face bathed in impenetrable dark. It is said that, given time, human beings will grow accustomed to anything, and so it was that Malina grew accustomed to her otherworldly visitor; still fearful, but as the months stretched into years, she would even manage to sleep on some of those nights. Her mind, already finding the abuse formulaic, would drift off into vulnerable safety.

Unfortunately, the illusion of security would not last. As any master tormentor would tell you, true pain cannot be induced in an unprepared subject; a victim must first know suffering, and then believe it to be over. They must believe they can survive it, surpass it; so it is that true darkness only exists underneath light; true anguish only exists underneath hope.

It happened right after her sixteenth birthday, at a big summer event that all of her classmates and friends were attending. More importantly, however, a certain boy would be making an appearance; a boy that, whenever he would occupy her conscious mind—a common occurrence indeed—would lead her cheeks to blush and her chest to rise as if filled with a fiery heat. It was at this event that she would gain enough confidence to approach him, and it was at this event that she would share her first youthful kiss under a cedar tree, a passionate moment that would solidify itself in her memory, a reminder of the shining golden years of her childhood, a certainty that...

No, something was wrong. It was a feeling that came with a familiarity, like when you find yourself alone, yet cannot shake the feeling that you're being watched — a tingling on your back so primal, raw, and forceful, that every cell in your body screams at you to get out, *get out now*.

She opened her eyes, slowly, warily, the light of the summer sun momentarily blinding her, her reddish lips still firmly glued to the boy's in that awkward teenage way, but her gaze was not set upon her romantic partner. It went beyond, beyond the cedar tree, beyond the park and the narrow road that flanked it, went as if pulled there by an invisible leash to the underside of a nearby bridge.

It was an old bridge, forever cemented in local teenage folklore due to the many unexplained deaths that plagued its vicinity. Now the terror was very real; underneath the old concrete beast, in that dark spot where the sun's light just cannot enter, behind a rusted chain-link fence, stood a familiar shape.

It was the demon, her monthly stalker. This time it felt different—it *was* different—for the demon was facing her; for the first time, she could see its face clearly. Its head was bald, with skin layered in an unknowable milky complexion.

Great big sunken eye sockets orbited dark, empty eyes, pinpricks of purplish red light. Abnormally pointed ears emerged from either side of the scalp, and only featureless skin existed where a nose should have been. But all of this was overshadowed by the large, ear-to-ear smile, a grin so outrageous and preternatural in its form that it went beyond twisted ecstasy. It had no lips, and its smile seemed to stretch out of its face, an impossible fence of sharp teeth ever widening, ever moving, its edges roiling shadow, as if immaterial.

And there it stood, motionless except for the smile as it grew and grew and grew like a stain upon reality, consuming what little light graced it. She wouldn't see that boy ever again; she wouldn't kiss anyone else that year.

The sun's light is ever bright, ever strong, and so Malina, ever hopeful, eventually allowed herself to indulge in her desires again; a teenager that she had grown to love, Henry, became her first boyfriend at the ripe age of seventeen. The demon, as if banished by the aura of young love, retreated from its nightly attacks on her psyche and, for the first time in years, she felt truly happy.

It is said that you can miss the sweetness of candy only once the sweet itself has been plucked from your still savoring mouth, and so true despair can exist only after happiness—real happiness, at that—has been tasted. The Devil's whispered truths:

Loneliness is naught but a weak, infirm disease. It cannot infect a healthy heart, so it ever lies in wait, shadow in your step; oh, how it prances and howls in glee whenever you find love.
Yes, there's never existed a better chisel than love for the gem that is the human heart; how easy it is when you're in pieces, how simple to sneak in. So quickly you seek to rebuild, giving no second glance to what you are picking up.

So the demon came again, this time seeking her whenever she was without him whom she loved, whispering poison directly into her ears from the shadows of her room, from the gloom-ridden storm drains, and from behind her as she walked home at night. With its horrible gurgle and screech it would whisper, like a demonic litany, a single word over and over again:

"Jennifer..."

Each instance of fright turned to hatred and disdain; she did not understand who this person was — why was this beast from the depths of the abyss whispering some poor girl's name time and time again? Jennifer, Jennifer, Jennifer, Jennifer, *Jennifer.*

"Who the hell is Jennifer?!" she would loudly beseech the shadows; as usual, they would simply cackle back in mockery, never bestowing an answer, her mood ever souring from this new form of unknown torture. This continued for a few months,

until one fateful day, just as suddenly as it had come, it went —
back to silence, back to peace.

It is said that everything that begins must end. Despite her
best efforts, Henry and Malina naturally grew apart; one gray
autumn afternoon, their fairytale love affair formally ended and
the magic all dissipated.

Malina's life became a churning whirlpool of sorrow. The instruments had begun to play her tone again, but the notes were
all wrong—a maelstrom of D minor, setting the stage for the
fiend's master plan—as when she was exiting her classroom, she
serendipitously overheard two of her classmates talking:

"Hey, isn't that Henry's girlfriend? What was her name, Ma-
linda or something?"

*Pulse accelerates. All instruments begin to rise in intensity. The
trombones let out a grim groan. Stage lights focus on Malina, bathing
her in a dark blue hue.*

"Are you crazy? Henry's with Jen right now, and going strong
from what I hear..."

*The violins kick in, frantically scratching higher and higher notes.
All wind instruments cease; stage lights change focus to the two girls.
Lights shift to a brighter hue; the curtain is about to drop.*

"Jen? You mean Jennifer from religious studies class?"

*One last, long, shrieking E-string drone from the strings. Percussion
ends with an aggressively loud middle-C strike of the wood block.*

"Mhm."

*The curtain drops. The lights on the stage turn a hellish red. The
violin and cello play that last note as long as possible. End of the first
act.*

Malina's mother was concerned that night. She knew the

breakup had been rough on her daughter, but on that eve, the house was plagued by a grim cacophony of sorrow: deep, guttural cries, overlaid by spurts of maniacal laughter — laughter summoned from the deepest pits of despair, a comic horror possible only once someone peers into the intricate lines that lie behind the curtain of the tragicomedy that we call life, and punctuated occasionally by the despondent cries of the truth.

And that night, the beast came again. This time, and for all the times thereafter, it looked straight at her — marveling, in nearly orgasmic pleasure, as she writhed in the most brutal of emotional torments.

Don't fix what ain't broke is a very simplistic adage. It offers primordial, yet relevant, wisdom: if something is working, let it be. But on some level, it stifles creativity; just because something is working doesn't mean that it couldn't be working *better*.

Idle hands are the devil's workshop is one more nugget of old sagacity. Stillness of the body and mind causes stillness of the soul, and nothing but evil can grow in such monotonicity; yet on some level, it severely undermines the sheer tenacity and industriousness required to perform the lowest acts of evil.

Therefore, the demon—ever the primal sage—labored endlessly in the dark between the stars and streetlights, always perfecting its abhorrent craft, formulating its schemes. It had discovered that the seed of desperation was already sown in Malina's psyche, and there was no need to worry, for desperation is a strong and resilient weed, only needing sporadic nourishment.

And so their macabre song and dance evolved further. Any time Malina would have the slightest negative experience related to a sexual matter, even something as trivial as walking home alone on Friday night because she couldn't approach that boy across the bar, it would be there. But how could she? The few feet that had separated them became an immeasurable distance, to be crawled over while weighed down by the chains of trauma.

Hence, *it* would approach *her*, and begin its unscrupulous verbal assault, watering that blistering seed with the most toxic of poisons: "Of course you're alone — you're *pathetic*! Of course you're walking home without him, what did you think was going to be different? Do you think he would have *liked* you? *You?!* How could anyone ever like *you*?"

It would cry out in its frighteningly penetrating voice, a voice that would go through muffling earphones and grasping, terrified hands — a booming, scratching sound that ripped through her senses and invaded the deepest recesses of her mind.

She would run into a bus, hoping, praying to anything that would listen to, please, just allow her to escape this torment for one second — only to find the monster sitting on top of the roof of the car driving beside her, smiling, waving:

"Pa-the-tic!"

"*Pathetic!*"

"Pitiable, pitiful, piteous!" it laughed, gargling that dark liquid. "What do you suppose your 'friends' are talking about right now? Me personally, I think they are most likely making fun of how much of a sad, disgusting piece of shit you are, don't you think?"

She would run crying and wailing through the night; it would follow, appearing in her reflection on decorated windows as she crossed the deserted shopping district. "Yeah, nobody likes you

— how could they? How could *anyone*?!"

Eventually, she would run into her dark and dirty apartment, quickly glancing at the red moon with cowering eyes, only to find the abominable creature's spindly, dark-painted nails wrapping around it, like a killer's deft hands ready to choke and strangle a fair neck.

Inside her home she would run, she would sprint—almost instinctively—to her bed. She would throw herself onto it, seeking comfort, seeking any sort of warmth — but the sheets were, as always, cold. And tonight, the demon continued, standing now in the middle of her bedroom:

"Malina..."

"Malinaaa..."

"*Malina!*"

She looked over, her soul crushed, her eyes glazed over.

"Do you think he moans her name when he fucks her? Henry, I mean—you think he screams *'Jennifer!'* in pleasure as they both climax, lovingly embracing each other?"

An electric current ran through Malina's spine. She was at her breaking point; there was no more, not a single morsel of torture she could endure before...

"I mean, it's Friday night!" it said, almost quizzically, before laughing again. "They're probably doing it right now, probably right in the middle of..."

It stopped, for the first time in a very long time shut down by pure, unadulterated interest. Malina had stood up and reached the kitchen, and now stood provocatively, aggressively, with a large kitchen knife in hand.

"What are you doing with that? Will you use it on me? Or

will you use it on yourself? Will you really cleave your flesh, your bone, your future? Have you finally given up?"

She allowed the blade to hover over her wrist, tentatively, hand trembling, as the demon spoke again. "You never know when things might change. Things could always get better, Malina. I mean, everything that's happened so far has been your fault, but you could always improve, right? But who are we kidding? There's no point in lying to yourself. You know you'll never go through with it because you're weak — because you *are*, and always will be..."

She started screaming at the top of her lungs: "*No!* Don't say it, please, please stop. I can't hear that word another time!"

"*Pa*—" The smile widens.

"—*the*—" Hollow eyes, like dead stars, grow brighter.

"—*tic*."

"*Why?* Why are you doing this to me? Why have you tortured my whole life? Why do you keep coming back? *Why me?!*"

And for the first time there was a change — the demon's smile disappeared. What had always been an unshakeable grin had reversed into what could only be described as a frown.

Its whole facial structure was now contorting. Its features wrinkled — skin, muscle, and bone groaning and cracking, as if made of clay, into a gloomy expression. The demon looked sad, as if something Malina had said had truly hurt and upset it to the depths of its core. It raised a bony claw to its chest, mimicking a stunned gesture. And thus it spoke, with—for the first time—a tear-jerked gasp of sadness in its rasping gurgle:

"Because I'm *your* demon."

A loud metallic clunk reverberated against the walls of the

now-silent apartment as the knife fell to the floor, and two muf-
fled steps followed suit as Malina approached her lifelong op-
pressor. Her visage clouded in darkness, she inched closer and
closer until she was face-to-face with the towering entity, the
smell of blood and sweat permeating the air around it like a
drowning, pungent fog. Unfazed, she wrapped her arms around
the creature and—in one swift movement—hugged the monstrosity.

A sound like splattering liquid accompanied streaks of blood
now running down her back and onto the floor, crimson rivers
slowly painting the white canvas of her back. The creature had
hugged her back, tightly, digging its claws deep between her
shoulder blades.

A pale, reddish-silver sliver of fresh moonlight entered the
room, dancing around the shades to the tune of laughter, slowly
uncovering the faces of the two figures hugging intensely, two
blank and pale facades radiating a pure and honest smile.

An Empty Bottle

A bar is many things: for some, an unbridled source of comfort; for few, a home far from home; and, for others still, the source of all sorrowful mornings. Yet, in between cheers and served beers, there is always a fixed point, a midway of negativity so dense that it is all but palpable. One can taste it, sour and tarlike, among the cocktails and cigarette smoke.

Have you ever been to a bar, dear reader? I imagine you have, the staples of our civilization that they are. It is said that one of the first communal buildings the Sumerians built in ancient Mesopotamia was a tavern. Along with this first frivolous establishment came the first unhappy marriage, of course, although that is a story for another time.

If you have indeed been to such a pillar of human activity, then you must at least be "once-glance" familiar with the stereotypical crowd that can be found there. Now, I am not one to usually get in tune with stereotypes: it is typical for a stereotype to present a behavior so characteristically absurd of typecast caricatures. But it is undeniable that it is easy to find the following classes of patrons in every establishment.

Topping off the list is our belovedly-hated belligerent drunk,

a confrontational individual that sometimes presents a psycho-
logical duality, sober versus inebriated, that rivals that of Dr.
Jekyll and Mr. Hyde. Following him is his opposite, his yin,
for there must be balance: the overly-friendly drunk, a being so
overflowing with intimate friendship that his desire for physical
contact cannot be dissuaded even by a Stalinist soviet's granite
stare.

Between these natural forces of good and evil lies—as in the
very cards that so accurately foretell our future—the joker. An
entity whose (sometimes already considerable) entertainment
powers undergo an ascension into comedy heaven, revealing to
those in reach of their voice the ethanolic promethean flame of
"a really good fucking joke", something that will surely get repeated with other friend groups or at Sunday's family barbecue.

Nevertheless, there is a spot far more important — a place
always filled by the most colorful of individuals, and the focus
of this gallant tale: the sad chair. And I do not mean this in a
demeaning or hyperbolic tone — the sad chair is not a mere
moniker attributed to a particularly hideous piece of furniture,
although that very well may be the case. It is so much more.

For the sad chair is that void I described in the beginning; it
is the point in the establishment where all depressive thoughts,
words, and ideas naturally drift to, like some sort of pessimistic
gravitational maelstrom. You'll surely know the spot — a dirty,
half-broken stool near the corner of the counter, partially illuminated by swinging dingy lights. All too close to the restrooms
and the backrooms, and as such, ever populated by the poignant
aroma of regurgitated regrettable meals and overbearing sani-
tation products. That Godforsaken piece of sitting furniture —

adorned, as if in mockery, by a crown of stains so diverse in color and thickness that van Gogh himself could have painted them.

The sad chair has such a pull — it instills such a drive in all unhappy individuals in its vicinity that, inevitably, like the setting of the sun, a patron will be tempted to choose that spot as their resting place for that night, free to conjoin their negative feelings with the chair, feeding the ever-growing maw of darkness.

Specifically, there is someone very dear to me who once populated the sad chair of every bar he visited during a most tumultuous period of his life, where his lover and future fiancée had left for greener pastures, leaving in his mouth naught but cinders; and so, to wash them down, he drowned in liquor. Shame the taste remained. His name was Jeremiah.

Now, so dark was this chapter of his life, so deep had he regressed into self-loathing, that he was sleeping with a hangman's noose tied neatly around his pillow.

And so it was, on that fateful Wednesday night—the loneliest night at any bar—that Jeremiah went out to peruse his favorite establishment, wallet brimming and fattened like a Christmas pig, ready for consumption and depravity. It was when he entered this establishment, however, that the tale truly began. For, as his bloodshot eyes — those red glass bulbs, already moistened with the first of many tears — scanned the dimly-lit, smoke-filled room for his spot, they came upon something most unusual: his spot was occupied.

Now, it is something rare indeed that more than one patron every night desires—or is absorbed by—the sad chair. It is customary, in the sadness line of work, to perform a subdued ritual of depressive acknowledgements. You see the spot occupied, ponder for a moment, perhaps silently lament the individual's circumstances... and promptly leave to find your own somewhere else.

But Jeremiah did not follow form that day. No, indeed, he broke the unspoken rule — and, in a moment that will forever be engraved in the hall of fame of alcoholic heaven, he approached the taut man sitting atop his stool.

If Jeremiah can be described now (and even more so at that moment) as an uninteresting man, the man currently occupying the sad chair was outwardly twice as unremarkable — short, chubby, his hair and beard long, dark, and unkempt. He wore a dark green jacket and ripped jeans, coupled with ordinary dad shoes — an overall aura of not wanting to stand out.

Yet, as Jeremiah inched closer, perhaps ready to tell this man to move seats, his gait slightly faltered when he noticed two very important—and very interesting—details. For one, the man had in his right hand a bottle of hard herbal akvavit — a most powerful forgetting potion... and the bottle was completely empty. Drawing his gaze up to the taut man's eyes, he was similarly struck by the irises' hazel color, tired and sunken in bloodshot sclera like his own. But as their gazes met, they both came alive: for a split second, the entire universe was set upon those two pools of brackish water, a reflection of all creation shooting up from the liquid, a gaze so strong yet soft that it seemed to harmlessly penetrate Jeremiah, like an infinitely thin needle through the heart of his soul. Jeremiah wondered what one must experience in order to have eyes like that...

It was only then that Jeremiah noticed that the man was considerably older, seemingly in his sixties compared to Jeremiah's twenties. The man held his gaze as Jeremiah finished his approach, apparently expectant of whatever Jeremiah had come to ask.

But all his words escaped his heart and his voice fell quiet once he noticed gold ring, an obvious token of engagement, on the ring finger gripping the empty bottle. It was right at this pivotal instant—with all time stopped inside the cramped, dirty cube of a room—that the words formed by themselves in Jeremiah's throat: "What is the purpose of life?"

The old man frowned, but kept silent, as Jeremiah pointed at his ring. With heavy tears in his eyes, he continued:

"Everything ends... even the longest meal has dessert, but what am I supposed to do afterward? What is the point of loving so deeply you dive into it, only to find yourself alone in that ocean of tears, unable to swim, shackled by unbreakable memories?" His head jerked violently as he spoke. "And I try, I try, I try, I try... *I try!* But all I can see are the knot's ends, the last pages in my future, and the sweetest ones of my past... so what's the purpose of life, old man? For all that this life has shown me is that the purpose of life is to end."

It was then that the old man spoke, with a hoarse voice roughened and treated in the fire of a thousand packs of cigarettes, yet carrying a sickly sweet aftertaste, not God-given but learned, through a long and undoubtedly interesting life. With a gaze unblinking and unshaking, he said:

"Why mustn't life be all that simple? Cast beyond the gated line, I urge the eternal struggle to reminisce and push me forth into endless, blissful nothingness.

A full ride to the edge, flowered pain riveting throughout my
senses, killing me to immortality!
Live! Live for living's sake, enjoy the mistake — that universal
flaw we call consciousness!"

Jeremiah was speechless. No more words were shared that
night, only tears—a cascade of sobbing—as two strangers, perhaps in name but not in soul, hugged tighter than brothers. It
was a long hug; bound together, they melded their inner selves
and all their bottled-up emotions, that dam of unspoken raw
feeling suddenly collapsing from the simplest of gestures.

They were cleansed, reborn — perhaps only for now, but reborn still; and, for the first and only moment in human history,
the sad chair of a run-down dive bar became the happiest spot
the whole town over.

Jeremiah never learned his name. He remains ever unchang-
ing in his memory — his personal, anonymous guardian angel.
This was, of course, many years ago; Jeremiah changed course
immediately following the auspicious encounter, his emotional
sails strong with renewed wind. He mentions sometimes that
he assumes the old man has already passed away, but he always
smiles and adds: "Maybe after I left that bar he got another bottle, filled himself up again with that acidic, painfully clear liquid,
turning his insides to bile... but I like to think not. I hope his
bottle remained empty. Empty and dry, so he could fill it with
joyful new memories."

The Ethics of Coin Tossing

"Why did you do it?" were the first words uttered by senior psychologist Dr. Jin. A psychoanalyst at heart, Dr. Jin had spent countless hours—and countless more glasses of his favorite dry English Gin—pondering. He had a lot of time to ponder and think, and this he had realised fairly quickly — for the bureaucratic purgatory one had to sit through to meet with Professor John D. Raimond, infamous serial killer, was nothing short of legendary.

He had spent months holed up in his small Rhode Island study, a dimly-lit office space consisting of a simple oak table, black leather armchair, countless shelves inhabited by all manner of thoughts from Freud to Jung — and, of course, a maroon rug. What had once been a nest for psychotics, neurotics, and the clinically insane had become a brooding haven for his growing insecurities. This was, in part, accentuated by the constant letters from the criminal office detailing a "postponement of session" under their overused "safety and security revisions".

He had wanted, therefore, to fill the empty calendar with preparations for the long-awaited meeting — especially how he would introduce the question of *why*. It was the crucial inquiry, the only reason he was allowed to talk with the incarcerated professor in the first place, and what he suspected would be the magnum opus of his professional career. As seasoned as the oak that constituted his table, he knew the importance of subtlety when talking to a patient, the *essentiality of tactfulness* as he liked to put it. But as he approached the island's supermax prison complex, as the heavily-armed and armored guards escorted him through massive gates of solid steel, and as the gentle scent of the sea breeze was overtaken by the oppressive musk of old metal, his mind had gone blank.

This had culminated in him starting the destined meeting with the brusque and unfortunate "Why did you do it?" As soon as the words left his mouth, their embarrassingly amateurish nature filled him with a reddening sense of failure.

He was sitting on a white metal chair inside a sterilized white room, rows of fluorescent lights beaming down cold, deathly-pale light and incessantly humming — a disinterested, mechanical monotone that drilled the inner ear canal, as if haphazardly looking for a way to enter your brain. In front of him was a table, silver metal, a perfectly reflective mirror stained only by the large set of manila files sitting comfortably in the middle. A fisheye camera protruded from the ceiling like a drop of tar on a marble tile; the floor in front of him reflected the navy-blue uniforms of the two guards by the door, offset by the black M-16 assault rifles resting in their hands.

But Dr. Jin did not really focus on any of that, for his attention was directed—unintentionally but inexorably, as if drawn in by the primal presence of a black hole—toward the man sitting across from him. Professor John D. Raimond was large in stature, his size contrasting heavily with Dr. Jin's modest frame; like a caged grizzly, the professor was bound to his specialized chair via thick metal restraints around his wrists and ankles. Yet, even bound, his rough-hewn, powerful hands—hardly those of a scholar—gave Dr. Jin an uneasy shiver.

At odds with his physique, however, the professor's expression was gentle: more fatherly than violent, yet angular and rugged. Curly, graying hair and bushy, salt-and-pepper eye-brows populated his otherwise clean-shaven, sanguine face, tied together by a chiseled jawline and piercing sky-blue eyes. Jin had been told beforehand that, apparently, the only request by the professor prior to the face-to-face was to be shaved; "I prefer to be clean-shaven when giving a lecture," he had reportedly remarked to the guards. Jin could only describe his first impressions of the killer as a man of many contrasts.

"That is the question on everyone's mind, isn't it?" the professor uttered in his deep, soft voice. Like a rubber band stretched to its limits and let go, Jin snapped back to the present with a small look of shock and confusion.

"Your direct tone came as something of a surprise," the professor continued. "Most people don't dare bring up the subject of my killings or their reason with such..." he paused for a moment, musing over his next words, and smiling a large grin of victory as he found them, "*caustic acidity*. But that truly is the crucial question, doctor...?"

"Jin!" The answer came quickly and directly.

"Dr. Jin? A foreigner, I see, much like myself — an immigrant to this land," he laughed, a coarse crackle. "Kindred spirits already... I remember when—"

"Why did you do it? You had everything... By societal standards—by any measure, really—you had reached the *happy ending*," Jin interjected further, deflecting the childish attempt at derailing an already shaky conversation.

The professor grew distant, linear features bending and wrinkles twisting into a deep frown, yet there was no rage in his eyes. It seemed not an expression of anger, but of sheer frustration.

"Happy ending? Let me tell you, doctor, there is nothing as absurd as a happy ending," He relaxed his features slightly. "Now, do not mistake my words, there is happiness at the end of the tunnel; you finish your life's work, earn your awards and prizes, get the pretty girl and marry her before riding off into the sunset..." He looked up into the ceiling, reminiscing. "And you are happy! But what happens after that ride ends, and the sun inevitably sets? You see, doctor, there is never truly an ending, not until you die. Life just moves forward, and your victories turn sour as they fade into memories; you complete your life's work and find out that your life just keeps going," he looked back down at Jin, his eyes inquisitive but serious, "So what to do, doctor? Everyone yearns for success, yet what do you do after success? How do you fill the cold, empty seconds, those freezing droplets in the grand waterfall of life? Must you acquire a new goal?" he scoffed. "Ambition never goes away, and you are filled with the unknowable truth that you do not have the time on this earth for any other writings in the history pages."

Jin observed the professor wiggling the fingers on his right hand, trying to get a look at the unmistakable white faded marking around his ring finger; the professor, lost in his reverie, continued. "So I tried anything and everything to keep my mind from stagnation, and my ambition's flame from devouring me in its heat — hobbies, new career paths, even disciplines far removed from the field of physics... but every step I took seemed to be a trek downhill, into the daunting horror of truth. My time had passed, and all the new frontiers were set upon by the beast of youth. And as my hypotheses became theories that became fact, that fact was beset by new theories. The new transformed into the archaic, and soon, my life's work was archived in the history books by another's, merely a stepping stone..." His right hand had now twisted into a fist, a clump of flesh trembling from its own force, reddening its edges with unadulterated ire. The professor, noticing this, took a deep breath, and it dissipated as soon as it had come. He continued, a calmer hue to his words: "So I bought a gun."

Jin reached for one of the files piled neatly on the table, caressing it with his fingers as he gave the professor an inquisitive glance. "Was this when you started...?"

"Killing?" the professor quickly answered, a sly laughter behind his words.

Jin nodded. Again the professor smiled, two rows of perfectly aligned off-white teeth, a series of old marble tombstones weathered by age and turmoil. "No, God no, I'm not the kind of unhinged monster that immediately takes to discarding life and morals; no, doctor, the gun was for me!"

"For you? That's... interesting, yet I cannot avoid the obvious..." Jin interjected, bemused, shifting in his seat.

The professor laughed louder, "Yes, doctor, I'm still here... I assume your next question is: *why?* Why didn't he just pull the trigger and save countless lives?" Jin nodded, giving the professor his attention as he reached for a small notebook and pen from his black leather briefcase, an eager slyness in his movements.

"Well..." the professor began, plunging back into his nostalgic reverie, "that was the plan, doctor, using the revolver to scatter my gray matter all over the painting on my office wall. A new coat, that's where I hid it, you see? From my wife. But I hesitated; the countless doubts one gets when he has the tip of a cocked revolver in his mouth, the brain's last line of defence against self-deletion, an unimaginably strong wind of thoughts battering at your willpower, uprooting it... so I took it out. And that's when I saw it," he smiled at Jin.

"Saw what?"

"My coin collection. It was a meaningless hobby, taken up more as a social front than any real interest, but within lay a valuable Civil War coin, so I took it, like a starving, ravenous carnivore, and cried out to the heavens, 'WITH GOD AS MY WITNESS, IF THIS LANDS ON TAILS, I'LL BLOW MY FUCKING BRAINS OUT!'" he paused, noticing that his booming recollection had garnered the attention of the guards' rifles. Performing an apologetic bow, he continued: "So I flipped it — a perfect toss, the ringing of the coin like the toll of an angel's bell, coming to take me away. As I caught it, my heart pounded, the drums announcing my end. Tears welled up as I relaxed my grip and slowly opened my hand... this was it, the end of the line. The world twisted and churned, as if caught in a meat grinder, and all else in my vision faded..." He sighed, a deep, relaxing sigh. "*Heads.*"

Jin hummed, rubbing his beard in a rough philosopher's caress. "So you gave yourself a fifty-percent chance?"

"It's not about that at all, doctor — besides, I'm not that generous," The professor shook his head and laughed again. "It's about determinism; it's about fate."

Jin quickly scribbled notes on the blank piece of paper as he spoke. "Interesting... so you mean to say the result of the coin toss was deterministic, and therefore you would never have lost? But if that were true, you could have flipped it half a dozen times, and—"

"—and it would be the same. And so I did, doctor, I flipped that coin a dozen more times, sweating bullets and trembling all the while... a dozen clean heads".

Jin glanced at the paper again and tapped it with his pen. "That is... one in eight thousand, approximately."

The professor smiled, pleased with Jin's arithmetic capabilities "Well done, doctor! Yes, around a point-zero-one-percent chance of survival; and it got worse, for I repeated that exercise every day for the better part of a year. Every morning, after having my coffee, I would put the revolver in my mouth and flip the coin, and every morning, the coin nourished me with heads."

"Seems unlikely," Jin murmured, a skeptical look dominating his features.

"Not unlikely, doctor — *nearly impossible*; and, yet, when I would flip it for any other reason, tails would rear itself just fine. I even flipped it for my wife—out of curiosity, of course—and there it was: heads," The professor closed his eyes in satisfaction and continued, "In my newfound curious revelation, I understood that—for some reason—I was not supposed to die yet. So I took a stroll, partly to make sense of the maelstrom of thoughts, and partly to return the revolver — I didn't need it anymore,"

Jin gazed expectantly at the folder. The professor nodded, and—not wanting to waste precious time—Jin opened it to reveal an amalgamated recollection of the grisly crimes of John D. Raimond. "Yes, that day was the first one. The first time I corrected causality."

Jin took out a file and turned to a new page in his notebook;

he had not been allowed to bring a tape recorder into the session—"safety and security revisions"—much to his endless dismay. Therefore, in preparation, he had organized clipboards and notebooks, separated into sections for ease of re-reading; freshly armed with brand-new writing intent, he readied himself, and verbally nudged the professor to continue.

"As I was saying — that day, I took a stroll, and—in the more unsavory part of my journey, through a small alleyway—I found a young man. He lay on his side, a pair of needles sticking out of his forearm. I rushed to help him, and yet, an idea sprung to mind — a warm sunrise in the desolate, darkened field of creativity. 'What better way to test out my theory than this?' I thought. So I crouched down near the young man and flipped the coin. *Tails.* I laughed at the coincidence and flipped again. *Tails.* Now I was getting nervous; twice more I flipped, and twice more the coin heralded the reaper."

"Did you flip any more times?" Jin asked, a bead of sweat making its way around his glasses.

"No, doctor, there was no need; causality had given me a clear message, and the revolver in my coat pocket weighed heavier than ever. So I took it out and trained its sights on the young man's head. My hand was shaking and the gun rattled like a pit viper, warning me of its potential for death. I took a deep breath, my lungs seemingly endless in their capacity. With a loud click, I cocked back the hammer — and that's when the man woke up. He looked at me, immediately understanding his situation even through his drug-filled stupor. His hazel-brown eyes were sending me a desperate plea, a single tear their unspoken messenger. I stared into his soul, his sight bathing me in an overwhelming sense of nausea; I pulled the trigger, painting the trash and walls of the alley with the rouge shower of his vitae."

Jin finally released his breath; throughout the recollection, it had been held captive in his chest. With a few more wanting gasps he steadied his racing heart rate. The room had fallen deathly quiet, as if an icy blanket of miasma had been draped over it.

"So, your first thoughts were to test your theory on the poor man, not to lend assistance or call an ambulance? There must have been a payphone nearby," The doctor's words tore surgically through the uncomfortable stillness, behind their calm veneer a heterogeneous mixture of discomfort and professional fascination.

The professor shook his head in an energetic gesture, clearly frustrated by the question. "No, no, doctor, you still don't get it, do you? It wouldn't have mattered anyway. He would've overdosed and—"

Jin cut him off, surprising the professor. "Firstly, you don't know that, you base this on speculation—"

"Rightful speculation!" the professor interjected defensively.

"But speculation nonetheless," continued Jin. "Secondly, we all die eventually, through gunshot or old age; in the meantime, we live. We experience and influence the world, good and bad alike — to deprive that someone of such a chance, even if it is infinitesimal... *why?*"

"Because that's where his influence ended, doctor," the professor answered, slowly laying his hulking frame back, the metal chair creaking in protest. He continued to speak, the words now punctuated by a smile on his face, vigor and fervent conviction spewing from his eyes: "The future's not set in stone because there is no future, no past, no present. Time is not linear, my good doctor — I am dying and being born in the same instant. From a higher dimension, all of time is a single dot. Every event, no matter how miniscule or how great, is confined within this infinitesimally small dot, so, yes, I shot that kid right between the eyes!" he exclaimed, tapping his forehead aggressively with a powerful index finger. "In every possible universe, the kid still lays on his back, heroin in his veins. The coin still lands on tails, and I still stand over him with a loaded revolver, pulling the trigger."

Jin frowned. He understood the basic idea, but he was a psychologist, not a theoretical physicist. What interested him was not if what the professor said was even remotely true, but which unknown mechanisms and pathways in a person's brain may lead to such a bleak outlook on reality and ethics. He sought to divert the focus of the conversation — he was certain of the *why* of the crime, but now he needed to get to the *why's why*. "How did you dispose of the body?" he asked nonchalantly.

"I didn't." The response came so surely and quickly that it took Jin a few moments of thought to even understand and react to it.

"What?" He rummaged through his files. "Here!" He pointed, fervently, at a black-and-white picture of what had once been a young man in his twenties, now grotesquely mangled by the trash compactor in which he had been found. "They found his body a few days later in a trash processing facility in Brooklyn."

The professor's smile had now morphed his entire demeanor into a smug palette of self-assurance. "I never touched the body.

Not his, nor any of the other eighty-eight."

The doctor shuddered slightly at the mention of the professor's dementedly high kill count — eighty-nine lives, eighty-nine human beings extinguished by—

"Doc? Are you listening?"

"Yes, apologies. Please proceed."

"I am no hypocrite, doctor, I never once attempted to hide my killings, nor did I ever attempt to advertise them — I simply killed, unapologetically and painlessly culling those who were destined to be culled," He flicked a finger at the armed guards besides the door, a gesture that invited the slight raising of both rifles. "If law enforcement agencies wanted to stop me, I was not going to impede their work or protect myself, for I was already protected by causality; they would arrest me when the time was right, and until then, the very entropy of this universe would serve as my guardian."

"You simply got lucky," Jin answered, the professor's grandiose claims forming a tiny hairline fracture on his statuesque professional restraint.

"Call it what you will... luck, fate, destiny, or God's will. Even you must admit that the events at the factory strain credulity." He smiled, a hint of malice creeping into that professorial tone practiced over many decades.

Jin shuddered again at the mention of the factory. It had been the incident that propelled the professor into national—and international—news coverage, and, in the hearts of many, into the status of urban legend. From his pile of dossiers and binders, the matte black folder, plastered with markings reading "CON-FIDENTIAL" in red and white, screamed up at him. He had been briefed on this event in excruciating detail long before the meeting by a contact of his in the police department, one of those friends that you only ever really see in memory, culminating in the ambiguously legal acquisition of this folder.

He did not want to look at it again. He had opened it at home the very same day with the intention of studying the event thoroughly, but its contents, the pictures, the autopsies, the children... It was a memory that violently stung at the doctor's id to the point of nausea, unceremoniously helped by the droning of the lights and that ever-pervasive metallic scent. Thoughts now flashed in his mind like a cornucopia of hellish visions, grisly macabre tableaus. He turned his attention away from them, focusing his *self* back to the interview. "You said you knew you would eventually be stopped. If so, what did you feel when the arrest finally came?"

The professor broke eye contact for a second, mournfully staring at the spot his wedding ring had once proudly occupied. "It was a normal, uneventful morning almost a whole year into my journey. I had finished my morning joe and was ready to begin the now-routine post-breakfast flips when a loud crashing at the front door almost sent me flying. Shouting—my wife's horrid shouting—came from the living room as a dozen footsteps echoed around the walls, increasing in strength. I knew my time had come, but in my initial shock, I had dropped the coin. I fumbled for it frantically — a man dying of thirst searching for water would've been the image of calmness next to me. By the time I had found it, however, it was too late. My office door exploded in a shower of splinters and the dark gaping maws of multiple gun barrels stared me down."

He looked up, his pupils possessed of a small quiver, as if now engulfed in a long-forgotten sadness. "I never got to flip that last coin, even though the outcome is easy to guess, right, doctor? Say, you wouldn't happen to have a coin about you, now? Would you, doctor?" Just like that, the quiver was gone, replaced on the professor's face with an emotion the doctor was not all too familiar with: something akin to childlike excitement.

In that moment, in that very instant, Jin realized that he had been awarded a golden opportunity. The professor had not willfully answered his question, but the question itself had roused some long-forgotten regret, what could only be explained in Jin's eyes as a chink in the prickly armor of the professor's psyche. Rather than scrounging for water leaking out of a crack in a dam, Jin saw the opportunity to open the floodgates.

He decisively reached into his left pocket, procuring a modest black leather wallet, from which followed a dime. Franklin D. Roosevelt's silver face glistened authoritatively under the constant beaming of the overhead lights. He admired it for a moment, making sure the professor was similarly dazzled by its glow, then placed his wallet back into his pocket and set the coin on his right thumb.

The ringing of the flip was so sudden and contrasted so violently with the room that, for a moment, Jin thought he was about to get shot for breaking some unmentioned rule. Yet the coin flew through the air, arching a majestic silvery path across the thick air of the interrogation chamber. The professor's muscles tensed suddenly, awoken by a long-forgotten feeling of ecstasy; his jaw clenched, an addict getting a long-awaited shot after a decade of withdrawal.

The coin landed with a soft, anticlimactic thud on Jin's hand as he closed his fist, a movement so quick and so skillful that the result of the flip was, for the moment, completely obstructed to all.

"Show me!" the professor demanded, a sort of canine eagerness to his now-forward-slumped posture. "Show me!" he repeated, more intensely this time, causing the guards to quickly shoulder their rifles.

"No," Jin said, abruptly pocketing the coin.

The professor's lower jaw reached hungrily for the table as his mouth stood agape, a deep frown encapsulating two pinpricks of blue light now shining with anger. "What are you *doing?! What game are you playing?!* SHOW ME!" he roared like cannonfire, any semblance of decorum seemingly broken by this act, his torrential anger only held back by the sharp metal clicks of the rifles' safeties turning off. "Why?" He asked through gritted teeth, a churning wall of yellow tint, "Why won't you show me?"

"Because it doesn't matter."

Jin answered calmly, his words striking at the professor with more force than Jin could ever hope to produce physically.

"What did you say?" blurted the professor, more in disbelief than attempted intimidation.

"Because it doesn't matter."

Jin repeated. "This flip, this random roll, does not change the fact that you're in jail for what is very likely the rest of your life. And I don't agree with you, professor — you say the fact that the universe is deterministic is reason enough to abandon ethical judgment and forgo good and evil. In my opinion, if that were true, to live acknowledging morality would be even more crucial. If no choice influences the outcome, and choice itself is only an illusion, then why flip a coin in the first place? Why fill yourself with misery and stain your soul with murder? Make others' lives better, try to do good in every instance, because when nothing has inherent value, only what we believe in has any worth. And you chose to believe in murder. You could have gone the opposite way, seeing those destined to die and seeing value in every second they don't, turning those moments into beacons of happiness. I think you used determinism as an excuse. I think the world murdered your ambition and you tried to murder the world, its people, its future, and even its ability to choose."

The professor tried to play off his anger with a smile, gesturing to the guards to take him back to his cell. As he stood up to be escorted out of the room, he spoke, a tint of sadness piercing through his other emotions and surfacing as a sudden voice crack:

"Flip or don't flip the coin... the result would have been the same, doctor."

As he went over the door's bright, looming threshold he added:

"Tails it is, then."

Gedankenfick

This one smelled of candy: that overpowering aroma of bloated sugar that floods your nostrils every time you pass the corner-store candy shop — and she was ridden with it. Oh, how I hated the feeling of childhood nausea it gave me, and this happy-go-lucky college girl I found on a dating app was just exuding it from every goddamn pore.

Those were the thoughts that flew through my frontal lobe as I hastily made my way into the ramshackle elevator outside her apartment door. I looked at my watch, a silver Seiko on a leather strap. It was 6:15 P.M. Good, it would give me just enough time to cut across Tiergarten and reach my apartment to get ready for my next date. *This one would be a doozy,* I smiled.

My name is Emil. I am a 26-year-old German student living in a small apartment in the center of Berlin and I have a problem, an urge, an itch so incomprehensibly irrational and overpowering that to even mention it is to invite unimaginable discomfort. I want—nay, *need*—to kill a person.

This is not a newfound inclination, either. I have always had this "killer instinct", although I never really acknowledged it as such. As a little kid at a playground or birthday party, questions like *If I stab my friend to death right here and now, would the rest of my friends hate me?* or *If I kick the dog right in the ribs with all my strength, would Papa still love me?* would appear occasionally in my mind.

These were dismissed, however, as passing oddities of a singular mind. It was not until my freshman year of college that the thought *What if I really did that?* crossed my mind. And a thought like that, once given the light of day, once given a modicum of attention beyond its inception, can never be ushered away. Like a cancer, it grew in my mind; but it was a benign tumor, and I have been all too happy to furnish my brain to accommodate its ever-increasing size.

The question, thus, became one of how how to go about the business of murdering another human being; passing ideas of purchasing a firearm off the dark web or crafting some sort of homemade explosive crossed my mind, of course, but the itch, like a gourmet chef, rejected these hastily-concocted appetizers. It was too dispassionate, like pressing a button; it lacked something, something real and raw.

It was two years ago, when I was pondering this dilemma in bed, that an epiphany struck me. I wasn't after the act itself, I was after the thrill of reaching the point, like a masochistic Sisyphus rolling up the rock of death. I was an ever-hungry huntsman — always able to satisfy the craving, of course, but aware of the coming and going of pleasure that it would entail. *Especially* the going.

So it became time to concoct a plan. I needed a way to isolate a victim reliably, and in such a way so as to avoid arousing suspicion. Kindness always reverberated and gave better results with people, so kidnapping was out of the question. It was only after scrolling absentmindedly through my phone that I realized. "A dating app," I murmured. "A dating app!" The murmur rose to a jovial scream as I arrived at the perfect answer.

I had always been an attractive man — getting matches would be easy. From years of interaction with others, my people skills were outstanding, my mannerisms perfectly crafted, and my social acumen second to none.

And so the song and dance had been established. I would match with someone, boy or girl; easily and effectively seduce them using a script carefully produced after analyzing their profile (although my improvisational skills were not half bad); go on a date with them; continue the courtship until the inevitable invitation over to their place, during which I would fantasize about killing them. I would play with the knives in their kitchen, playfully grasp their neck from behind and think of all the ways I could kill, murder, and maim them should it fancy me; this, combined with the sex, soothed the burning itch.

I had considered using *my* apartment, but—aside from the obvious danger of having a victim over should my urge overpower me—my living space was a mess. Filth and dirt clogged the rooms, up to the point where seeing a spot of visible clean floor tiling was cause for celebration. Tall stacks of dishes with unused trash and rotting old dinners decorated the kitchen; unwashed and stained clothes littered the floor along with old cardboard and plastic. Even some used condoms could be seen. I made a point to take them with me after every date, of course, just in case my DNA could be traced.

I didn't mind it. It gave the entire apartment a very distinct aroma, a soft yet savory tint that was wholly unique to my home — my own little scent, something nice to disinfect me from the miasma of perfumes and body sprays my dates used.

Much like me, my two-room studio seemed neat and attractive from the outside; whenever I came out, I made a point to go out clean, groomed, sharply-dressed and even perfumed — and, just like me, no one could take a look inside. Nobody could see the truth — that behind my gray metal door and glassy blue eyes lay a field of decay and rot, a land populated by death and darkness, a filthy little hole of despair.

I had performed the dance routine for two years now. Two years of constant dates and late-night house visits, and through-out these two agonizing years I had edged myself to the break-ing point because, surprisingly, my kill count remained steady at zero.

But it was not enough; every denied kill as of late was leaving my soul wanting, every victim spared was making my skin crawl. Even in this last date, my kind facade had almost slipped, and I was so very close to choking her to death during our Netflix sofa-fucking session. Of course, I had managed to put it off as sexual inexperience, but it had been hard and she was angry... angry was bad. Angry people remembered in a negative light, and small details and connections they might otherwise have waved off could claim permanent residence in their temporal lobe.

Luckily, there were contingencies in place for when I needed to escape an apartment quickly and without raising suspicion. After installing a rootkit on my phone, I had altered my mes-saging apps to have easily-modifiable messages that looked—at a passing, simple glance—real.

After that, all I had to do was ask my mother to send me a message regarding a menial task like groceries or unimportant family matters during the date, then, in the bathroom, modify the message to say something along the lines of "Call me, your dad is in the hospital," or "This is Dr. So-and-so, your mother just had an accident". At that moment, I would show the text and apologize to my host from the bottom of my heart. I would suggest I stay despite the fact, at which point most people would begin to feel bad and wish me the best of luck while dismissing me from their home. It had never failed me before, and today—as I hastily left her apartment—would be no different.

The shaking of the elevator ripped me out of my daydream and, like an anchor, rooted me back in reality. Already I was getting stressed; surely she had noticed something strange about me, some discrepancy with my actions... was she calling someone? What if she was friends with one of my previous flings?

The thought stabbed at me like a red-hot poker, sweat forming in my armpits and on my forehead. *If one of her friends is a previous victim, then they could put together a pattern,* I thought. *The* police *could put together a pattern.*

And, just my luck, the urge was getting worse and worse. I thought I might actually *kill* my next date... no, I needed to do it, I needed to formulate a plan to do it out-of-pattern if I just... "Shit!" I said loudly. I couldn't think with that stupid candy smell clogging up my nose — why did that fucking whore have to use that candy smell? "*Shit!*" I screamed, punching the elevator wall.

DING!

The loud ringing of the elevator door jolted me awake again, ripping me out of my thoughts and tearing them apart. The elevator door slowly slid open, and I hastily donned my most inconspicuous, friendly expression, crossing my arms to hide my now-visible pit stains.

A young girl slowly came into frame. She was wearing a black dress and black painted nails, her hair dyed black, mascara and makeup hastily donned. The chains and rings completed the emo look so popular now with younger teens, drawing a sharp contrast with her *Hello Kitty!* backpack.

She entered and looked at the unpressed elevator buttons. "You going down?" she asked, with that monotone bored voice; I smiled and nodded. She sighed, rolled her eyes, and—in the same motion—pressed the ground floor button. With a mechanical whir, the soviet-era metal box began to make its way down.

The sigh was good; she obviously thought that I was an idiot, or a dork uncomfortable with even the minute presence of a woman. This was remarkably good. To be ridiculed was always better than to be feared; the people we made fun of always occupied a passing fancy in our hippocampus, soon to be pushed out by some new stimulus — that is, forgotten.

Perhaps I had made no lasting impression on her, but the same could not be said the other way around. I had all but gone back to my thoughts when I noticed her perfume. It was unmistakable — it shot out of her neck in droves and quickly flooded the cramped elevator like a gas chamber. It smelled like candy.

The previous one worn by my date had had a sweet, but disgustingly rough, tint of milky chocolate; this one, even though masked by benzoin, contained the subtle—but most aggravating—drag of caramel. My face reddened, my back tensed up and my pupils dilated. A thought had taken center stage in my brain now — an irrepressible thought that, this time, I could not ignore. I had to kill this girl.

It was beyond stupid, of course. Two years of planning, two years of meticulousness were about to be thrown out by one im-

pulsive decision. But it was not impulsive—it wasn't even a decision—because the only thing I could possibly do to this chemical
weapons expert choking me with her filth was snuff the life out
of her with my own two fucking hands.

The timing would be tight though. I had mere seconds to
act before we passed the next floor and risked more uninvited
guests on our ride; luckily, I always came prepared. Ever since
undertaking my first nightly escapades, I had bought—and always carried with me—a pair of leather gloves. All I had to do
was slip one on.

I took a nice, long breath, noticing that my left hand had been
clenched all this time, to the point where my nails were about
to dig too deep into my palm, causing me to bleed. I stopped
and relaxed my tension-ridden body. Looking at the girl gave
me slight relief — she was short, perhaps 150 or 155 centime-
ters. I figured she could not have weighed more than 50 kilo-
grams. Her neck, soft and glistening under the overhead fluorescent lights, looked like a thin plastic tube compared to my
hands.

Pure strength had never been my ace in the hole. I was strong,
don't get me wrong—stronger than average, perhaps—but I was
no bodybuilder or powerlifter, and my lean physique did not
improve the situation; still, with such a small and weak oppo-
nent, overwhelming force would do. By my estimate, in less
than five seconds I could have leather glove on hand and hand
on neck. After that, constricting and crushing her trachea and
carotid artery would be, ironically, child's play.

She glanced back and caught me staring at her neck like an
idiot; she looked away and shuffled a bit closer to the door. She

suspected something, and we had just passed the second floor. It was now or never.

I quickly took my black leather glove from my right pocket and, in a smooth, practiced motion, slipped it on my right hand. She looked back, her eyes suddenly wide with a rush of fear — but I would not give her a single moment to react or scream. My heart racing, and my right hand—as if spring-loaded—shot out towards her neck, missing by an inch and hitting the first-floor button.

The claustrophobic metal cage came to a sudden stop, unbalancing both of us; the doors were not even fully opened before I was jumping out like a cat sprayed with cold water. She looked at me, dumbfounded, her eyes betraying a hint of fear as the elevator remained still for a moment, the whole scene an indiscernible tableau to her. After a few agonizing seconds, the doors began to close again.

As they did, I smiled and pointed at my gloved hand. "Sorry, germophobe," I blurted out, shrugging and forcing out a dry, apologetic laugh. She stared at me down to the last nanosecond — stared with an even more puzzled expression as the elevator took her, and her candylike stench, far down the gaping maw of the old shaft.

I dropped to my knees, defeated, sinking into the darkest pit of jet-black depression — now I was definitely screwed. I had managed to stave off the urge one last time, that was true, but she definitely would remember this. One more unavoidable piece to the ever-growing pattern. She was a key witness now, and way too close in time to the previous fuck-up for comfort.

They would come to question me, I was sure now. The police and the media would come and break down the door to my house and then everyone, every single person on this planet would see the darkness and the filth and... and the real me.

I started crying and choking for air, my sobs accompanied by great big rivers of snot running down my face and onto the floor. I grasped at nothing and took my frustration out on the nearby elevator door, pounding and screaming between gasps, my hands bleeding and my head spinning.

Would everyone at work still be my friend? Would my family still love me, would my...?

Ding!

It was a different ring — not the sharp, high-pitched yelp of the elevator door, but a longer and softer screech. I recognized it immediately — my phone's notification sound had gone off. I searched around my pocket and hastily pulled it out. The device brightened as I hit the power button and a bubble of text appeared on my screen.

My heart skipped a beat. Slowly, my cries stopped, and I rubbed my eyes to clear them. It had been a close encounter, to be sure, but I had committed no crime — nothing to warrant an official investigation, anyway. To the rest of the world, I was just an eccentric, promiscuous young man, who—like all young men—sometimes makes mistakes.

I smiled and took a furtive glance at my silver Seiko watch — 6:16 P.M. My smile grew larger. I could still make it home in time for my date with the barista boy if I crossed through Tiergarten. I cracked my back and took a deep breath. Somehow I knew that everything would work out — next time would surely be when

I finally took that tantalizing step into criminality. Next time I'd kill my date, for sure.

I quickly ran down the remaining flight of steps and waited a bit to make sure the emo girl was gone. Then I walked outside, into the cool winter Berlin air. The sun had already gone away, and long-necked street lamps lit the road. I took a deep breath again and caught a whiff of the nearby trash accumulating at the street corner. *Delicious.* I smiled as I checked my phone:

Samstag

6:17

"Congratulations! You have a new match!"

Perfect.

Kissat

Cats are such wonderful and complex creatures. They exist in a state of utter, universal relaxation — as in, they seem to be permanently outside the cloying, obscure trappings that we may call fate, destiny, or whatnot. I myself, through my many wanderings, have made some outstanding connections with such felines — their spiky ears pricked up as, between bouts of harmonic meowing, they endowed me with wisdom known only to these tabby tottling toms.

Did you know that not all cats are hunters? Yes, it is quite the unfortunate generalization, but I assure you: there are some very well-read kittens, philosophers of catkind, who—just after the obligatory morning nap and afternoon siesta—engage in all manner of discussion and debate. It was one of these sleepy thinkers—a great big Maine Coon with whiskers that curved, snaked, and danced as it mewled—that told me the tale you're about to hear.

It was with great sorrow that it told this story. I feared its seemingly animated whiskers would prickle me if I were to ask why, and so I lay still as a calm pond—on my stomach, as cats do, of course—and listened.

This story's tragic protagonist was an unnamed feline living far in the northern wilds, where prey is scarce, and—lacking the resolve or bravado for such daunting hunts—many cats in the region made their livelihood by a sort of farming. This kitten in particular was the proud owner and caretaker of a big apple tree (it is a little-known fact that apples are a delicacy among cats of northern latitudes). He would trade those fresh scarlet beauties for goods and services with other cats, and even other species of animals — although such interactions were rare, and—as with all other interspecific dealings—shaky at best.

It was tradition to make all apple-related deals under the apple tree back in those olden, wilder times, when the world was just a bit younger and so naïveté and tradition in trade mattered — although it is fair to state that feline dealings today have hardly changed.

They would meet under the great branches and inspect the aforementioned tree. If the buyer found the timber in question to be well-kept and up to a certain standard, the deal would proceed to a small sampling — a tasting of sorts, finalizing in the exchange of goods.

Our protagonist cat had garnered quite the outstanding reputation of being a top-notch apple caretaker, with his great big tree (providing apples of the Amorosa variety) standing atop a great big hill overlooking a great big valley in Lapland. I must clarify that, although cats love apples up north, they cannot simply subsist on them. Call it a cruel twist of feline-kismet or kittymet; they simply require other produce to survive.

Everything went as it should have for our protagonist; before the last of the warm summer rays had breached the clouds, he had already—through apple dealings alone—stockpiled a sizable amount of food and commodities. He was the talk of kittytown, his luxurious gray-white fur flowing in the wind, as if gently stroked by some caring, invisible hand. He even had time to perform six daily naps instead of the usual four due to having already stockpiled enough for winter. It was—as many of my furry friends would agree—the ideal life for someone of feline disposition, the envy of all mouse-hunters.

But, if his life was perfect, why were his eyes dead?

His eyes—those great big blue orbs that through most of his life had been darting around curiously, searching and observing even the most minute of details—had now become still. A blue pond so still that it perfectly reflected all, and so no one noticed; to look into his eyes was to see naught but your own emotions shot back at you, a mask thin and smooth beyond porcelain.

This kitty had become afflicted with an illness that would not be given a name for centuries to come, an illness that thrives in a healthy body and tears apart the soul, an illness of the self.

He had worked tirelessly, day in and out, to achieve the perfect life and yet, now, he felt a pain that could not be expressed — a tsunami of negativity that rose up from his navel and churned his stomach, making him unable to eat, fearful that all that icy burning bile would come spilling out if he even attempted to open his mouth.

Some days, it was in his joints — creeping white worms that tangled his limbs and whispered into his fur, "don't jump," and "you can't make it". These were the good days, the days when the sickness had a semblance of form; most days it didn't — most days, it didn't whisper or assail him. Most days it just existed.

It lay dormant in him, neither hot nor cold, neither painful nor soothing. It just existed within, perfectly imbalanced. And that's all it took; the sickness had taken residence in his soul and frozen it, yet he felt nothing. And that was the problem — he had been sick before, and now wished that his pain were definite, a scratch in an arm that he could cut off. It hummed asleep, a cacophony of silent wails, disorienting his every thought.

He tried to get better, he really did; he drank the herbal milk the cat-shaman offered, but it did nothing. He basked in the sun and prayed, but his mewling was monotone and stunted. When he was offered to join the weekly cat festivities—dancing, singing and mating—he declined politely, incapable of explaining how the sickness now made all feline interactions nauseating. To interact was to sink deeper into those perfectly calm, yet enraged, abyssal waters... yet deep below was nothing but more sickness — an endless loop, ever sinking.

And so he lashed out. Driven by occasional bursts of energy, he would run around his home, ready to change his life, only to be stricken once again shortly after. It was in one of these bouts of anger, however, that everything changed.

He was running around his house, mad like a rabid dog, when he found himself in front of his precious tree. He stared at it, in awe and trembling, for an idea was brewing inside of him — a dark idea, spawned out of desperation.

He didn't even consider it. Acting purely on impulse for the first time in his life, he jumped onto the side of his tree and, claws out, tore into its bark, gnawing a great big gash, meowing in pain as he ripped it up.

When the deed was done, the-once perfect tree trunk now bore a few distinct cat marks, oozing sap as they bled onto the ground. His heart similarly slashed with regret, he cried out in pain.

He cried out...

This was it. This was the first time in recent memory that he felt a pain he could recognize, a pain he could make physical, and so he opened himself and let this new wave of suffering fill his soul, momentarily crushing the sickness and freeing him.

That night he danced, he mated, he mewled, and he felt alive.

Had he finally cleansed himself of this dooming illness? The wounds on the tree turned to scars as the waters of time flowed ever forward, and the memory of the sickness became just that — a memory.

He had willingly defaced his tree, his livelihood — but he could hide it. Somehow, he had to hide it, or he would be ruined, but he had options. They were just a few scratches on an isolated part of the tree — he could use a tarp, or some sort of cloth, and excuse it as style or husbandry. And so he did.

But as winter closed in, days blended together into night, the waters of time sped faster than ever, and the suffering of brutalizing his tree had faded into memory. His soul was fresh and new... perfect for the sickness.

It came again, this time even harder than before, as if angered by what he had done — and this time, it used the tree against him, tormenting him with that uncaring, constant humming, flooding his soul until the black tar spilled out onto every organ and tissue, sickening them as well.

He desperately grasped at the memories of hurting the tree,

but they did nothing. The sickness was resistant, and so a new bout of hell began.

His worried friends and family sent him again to the shaman, who only recommended light exercise in-house and more herb-infused milk. They didn't know... they knew nothing and yet they tried to interfere. "Get better," — *as if I could just will it away!* "We're here for you," — *as if you could ever share in my misery while having your soul free! Liars, traitors, laughing behind my back... had they discovered the tree? The tree?!*

And so he went again, and for a second time he committed that horror; he elated in blissful agony as the chains of suffering around his soul went from formless to definite.

The cycle had been formed, an ouroboros that never offered an escape, only a temporary sanctity that was easily broken — and, in the end, only fueled the sickness, for pain can never heal pain.

Scars turned to trauma, and eventually, he was unable to hide his tree any longer. Word quickly spread throughout northern cat society, and all the future dealings of his apples faded away into excuses and apologies; this winter he would survive, but the next one... who knew?

He had been banished — not officially, of course, but every other cat knew. Every other cat judged, and every other cat found guilty.

For who would willingly damage their own tree, scar the bark and violently defile it? Only a madman, bereft of reason and utterly deranged, right? And a deranged cat cannot be allowed to exist in society — civilization belongs to the sane, the normal.

But then again, how many other farmers, their souls stricken with heavy, icy stakes, would willingly tear up their trees if only for the warmth of their sap to melt them?

Are these little kittens to blame? Or is it the ice and snow, the long nights and dull, gray days? Or is it the belief that the scratches on a tree's bark can have any influence on the quality of the fruit that it will bear?

Γ — Final Act

CHARACTERS

IXION (The Protagonist)

CHYSANTHOS (The Mugger)

THE VOICE (Narrator)

(There is no sound as the lights come on. The curtain rises. The Voice is sitting centre-stage on a park bench, donning white robes. They have a serene expression about them; unbothered by the audience, they unfold their arms, bow authoritatively, and at once address everyone in the theatre. There is no sound but their voice, accompanied by the gravitas of its very meaning, an unheard soundtrack for their poignant words.)

THE VOICE: You are not real. (They pause for a moment, letting the confounding weight of their words set in before continuing. They stare far away, at the back of the theatre, never making eye contact.) You will be given a moment, a snippet of a person's life, and although you can see them and they may see you, you are not real. (The Voice now stands up, slowly and meticulously, as they continue their address.) Many things are not

really real, and yet we cling to them, speak to
them, seek comfort in their words; but, as with
all things unreal, you must remain silent. (They
take their index finger to their puckered lips
and hush the audience, still not looking at any
particular member, their gaze infinite and lost
in the back. Then they smile solemnly.) It is
crucial that today you remain silent and seated;
otherwise, you would become real, and all would be
lost. Fare thee well... and good luck... (They
finish their address and slowly exit stage left.)

(Just as The Voice has walked off stage, Ixion
appears, a lit cigarette in her mouth. She wears a
leather jacket, jeans, and some black makeup. She
looks tired and is walking home. There is music now,
an inquisitive, playful piano accompanies Ixion's
footsteps from side to centre-stage. She takes
periodic, almost robotic, huffs off of her cigarette
until, at centre-stage, she flicks it onto the stage
and unceremoniously steps on it. She pouts, her eyes
darting from side to side as she speaks to herself,
the piano dying down.)

IXION: They can't just... replace me... can they?
I mean... (She looks to the floor.) I created
this band! It was my idea, and these assholes

want to take it away from me? (She slowly walks to
the right side of the stage. The piano is back,
softer and higher-pitched. Its inquisitiveness
remains, but it now carries hints of melancholy.
She continues speaking as she walks.) The name...
that was mine! The goddamn chorus, mine as well!
Who do they think they are... taking my shot,
my...

(Suddenly, a violin comes in, high-strung and
screeching like a wounded animal, as Chysanthos
enters the stage from the left. He is disheveled,
a dirty, ragged jacket covers his torso and hangs
over his torn pants. It jerks Ixion back from her
mind. She looks around, confused, until she looks
at Chysanthos. He approaches, slowly but surely,
passing the bench on his way as she takes a closed,
defensive posture. He stops a few steps away.)

IXION: (To Chysanthos, dismissively.) Look, man,
    I've had a shit day, so whatever you want, I ain't
    buyin'...

CHYSANTHOS: (He has a twitchy feel about him, like
    a stormcloud congested with lightning and ready
    to explode. He looks around, wary, a couple of
    times until he speaks. His voice is ragged; he
    stutters and slurs his speech.) I need to take

a... t-t-train home... don't got e-e-enough for
the t-t-ticket... can you help... m-m-me out?

IXION: (She is bothered. She looks back at him with
a hint of disgust and takes a step back. The piano
plays a discordant deep note, fearful) Hey, man,
sorry. I don't have cash on me...

(The violin is back. A predatory but slow note
appears, humming.)

CHYSANTHOS: (Stepping forward and signaling eagerly
with his hand as he looks around again.) Your
ph-ph-phone and wallet th-th-then! (He commands
impatiently, his hands grasping eagerly.)

IXION: (Stunned by the demand, appearing fearful as
she frantically looks around.) What?

(The violin screeches its warning, notes sharp and
metallic. It is accompanied by an adrenaline-inducing
rush from the piano.)

CHYSANTHOS: (Pulling out a knife.) The fucking phone
and wallet, you BITCH! (He takes another large
step forward. The knife, small but ever daunting,
sharply refracts the hues of the stage lights all
over its metallic edge.)

(An aggressive debate begins now between the violin
and the piano. They both extend their notes, as if
warning the storm closer.)

IXION: (Gasping loudly, her eyes transfixed on the
    object as she begins to hyperventilate.) Wha...
    what...? No... I... please... (She begins to
    fumble around in her purse. With a shaking hand
    she removes her phone, extending it slowly to the
    mugger. Her quivering, dilated pupils stare at
    the blade once more, and her breathing, accompanied
    by fearful moans, accelerates further.)

(There is another sharp violin note. This time,
a high piano gasp tailgates it, as if startled as
well. Chysanthos lashes out, hand like a coiled
spring, as the silver of the knife cuts across the air
and Ixion's extended hand. She screams in surprise,
drops the phone, and begins rushing to the left of
the stage. All instruments go silent. Chysanthos,
angered, leaps after her. The lights go out as he
reaches her. Ixion screams horrifically, a series
of pained and anguished cries followed by the rushing
gasping of air leaving surprised lungs. Footsteps
are heard in the dark, hurried, as they disappear
towards the right of the darkened stage. Chysanthos
exits stage right. The lights come on.)
IXION: (Looking around, sobbing and hyperventilating.
    She is lying on her back, her upper body disheveled
    and covered in blood.) Wh... (Pained gasp.)

Where... am I? (She lumberingly drags herself to the bench, still bleeding and sobbing silently. She clambers up to the bench and slumps on it, sitting upright with much difficulty, grimacing in agony. She sits on the bench for a while, her eyes drooping. Sobs and moans come and go. At points she presses her lips or grits her teeth.)

(The silence is cut by a series of inquisitive piano notes, like flickering embers, now tentative towards a coming breeze. Ixion notices the audience, and her eyes widen in shock. She is afraid now. Mouth agape, her eyes lock onto the eyes of an audience member, then another, then another. As she does this, her hope rises, visibly. She musters the will to speak.)

IXION: (To audience.) Hello? (A pause. No answer.) Who are you people? Where are we? Why are you here? Look, I was mugged, some asshole... (With a pained groan, she struggles to speak.) I think he stabbed me... It hurts so much and I can't feel my... my legs... Please call an ambulance... I... I think he took my phone. (She breathes heavily as she waits for an answer.) HELLO??? (Her voice is much louder, her face contorted now by fear and a silent plea. It doesn't stay silent for long.) Look, please I... it hurts so much,

please help me! (She points to her wounds, and now looks for the audience member nearest to her.) YOU! Please, can you help me? PLEASE! (She begs now, crying. She hastily crawls off the bench, landing roughly and screaming in pain, composing herself as she approaches the audience member, going as close as possible without climbing off the stage, unable to. Her voice is now a blended storm of fury and desperation; she shoves her hand out from under herself. It is covered in blood. She brings attention to it, placing it in between herself and the audience member.) See?! I think I'm bleeding out, oh please! Why won't you answer? Why do you just sit there, you asshole?! Why do you just watch?! (She begs the audience as a whole again, breaking down into tears as she repeats the phrase loudly again and again, a funerary mantra.) Why won't you answer? (She rolls onto her back near the edge of the stage and laughs while rivers of tears stream down her face.) I'm going crazy... or I died, and I'm in hell... (She looks at the audience and laughs again, making the motion of playing an electric guitar with her hands.)
(The same string she plucked in her imagination resonates throughout the theater: a high E.)

IXION: This would make for an interesting song...
    (She puckers her lips and sarcastically recites an
    improvised verse.)

    Hate, loathe! Sprites-a-many, hate and screech
                    your judgment.
    Look at me, stake your glistening coals, pass your
                    judgment!

    (She looks around, then closes her eyes.)

                    Why do you stay silent?
                    Why do you just stare?
                    Am I your entertainment?
                    Must I dance-ah?
                    Fool-a-fool-a-fool's tidings, yeah
                    To get you to answer?

IXION: (With a wry laugh.) I always got the good
    ideas... way too late, still... (To the audience.)
    I don't know if you assholes are real, or just
    in my mind, but I keep getting flooded by these
    memories, memories... and a silent crowd... I
    used to be a little shit in middle school... (She
    smiles, reminiscing.) Always playing hookie or
    sneaking off to go listen to some oldheads play

guitar down at the... (She looks up.) The
square. Yes, they'd all gather, drunk and high off
God-knows-what and just play. They had nothing.
Saw a couple of 'em rob a store off the freeway
just for breakfast, yet... (She closes her eyes,
melancholic.) They'd let me hold on to it, give
it a spin, their precious baby they had somehow
managed to cobble together, that scratched-up old
thing... (She smiles.) I held it like it was
the holy grail... (Hands grasping weakly in the
air, she looks at her bloodstained palms.) In my
church, Jesus and the Devil, hugging banging heads
to Broken-Hearted Blues. (She pouts again.)
(The beginning of ''Nannar's Lament'' plays now.)
IXION: I was bottom-of-the-barrel, dirt-poor, and
yet every time they played I had a banquet. I'd
go to sleep, my stomach flat, yet I felt fat, rich.
(She sobs a bit. ''Nannar's Lament'' resumes playing.)
Until I was... rich. Had it all, my shot at being a
legend was right there! And those assholes want to
take it away from me? (She begins to stand up and
falls back down, wincing.) Oh right... I'm dying...
Why am I on the ground, alone? Where is Joanne?
Why are you here? (She looks at the audience and
cries until ''Nannar's Lament'' ends.) I am not alone.

The inside of my skull is populated by sprites, (She
gives a dry, pained laugh.) yet they only strip me
bare... YOUR EYES ARE HURTING ME, CAN YOU NOT SEE?
(She continues reciting an improvised song, her eyes
slowly closing as her life flickers.)

> Please I beg - no, I beseech, no, no, no
> A hungering man's supplications!
> A meal, tantalizing as it may be
> No word consumes the pain - isolation.
> I beg of all those who sit to have mercy
> To torment would be to love
> I cannot stand it, this solitude
> This horrid wilting lack of wilting.
> I am alone,
> Yet all that I ever prayed for
> Uncompromising crowd
> A never-ending concert.

(As the song is halfway done, Ixion stops emphasizing
words and her intonation falters, monotone and ordinary.
Rhyming ceases as the last words are barely slurred
out. Her eyes begin to close as the lights and
curtains do the same. There is no music. The lights
go out; the curtain falls.)

Nannar's Lament

Lost Sheet

Nannar

52

56

61

65

"O My Lecherous King"

Last days of summer
"The peasantry is rife with sin; they are of dark and of dirt.
They want for that which they cannot have, and have desires
for all they want."
— Adage of Nobility

The Normans had built a palace; it was as rich and dominant as it was vast, and it had a thousand rooms. There was no throne, not in the traditional sense; the king of the island, ruler of the palace, sat alone in his study, waiting patiently for the day's petitioners to arrive. It was early in the morning, but these waking hours evidently provided no respite from the already overbearing summer heat. The royal chambers and study were situated at the top of the palace's tower, overlooking the capital city. Only the cathedral rose to such heights, and thus the world writhed beneath him, dirty and sweaty from the scorching sun.

His world, his dirt, his sweat. But the island *was* prosperous, all things considered, and it played an admittedly important geographical role in the matters of the grander world. And he was not an apathetic king — he had spent as much time as any royal might deign to appease the populace. A populace divided, cleaved through by the rugged edge of culture (or *cultures*, in this case). The foreign but wealthy mainlanders clashed all too often—and all too often violently—with the less privileged locals, whose roots were deep in the earth, deeper than sin or royalty...

"Petitioners," a kindly voice pierced the haze, drawing the king's scattered thoughts back up into the tower; it was his royal advisor. "The petitioners, sire — they will begin to arrive sh-sh-

shortly." The advisor composed himself, leaving a silver platter of foodstuffs and confections, and promptly left. The king sat upright on his cushioned chair and took hold of some pastries. As he ate, his mind shot off once again — *The ebb and flow of ruler-ship*, the king mused, mouth demolishing the sweet treats. *The monotonous but necessary drag to keep everything in order, to clean off the dirt...*

BANG!

Startled by the sound, the king looked around. He initially thought his advisor was back and had perhaps dropped a second platter. But the heavy wooden door to his study was closed, and not another soul's breath could be felt in the room. His mind recreated the sound, tracing its origin within the space of the study, landing most curiously at the large window right behind him. He turned around quickly, more intrigued than scared, and darted his eyes analytically, over the window, over the large blackwood cupboard, down the banisters and engraved stone pillars, ending abruptly on a small black object on the ground.

It was rectangular and thin, and its glossy surface reflected the stunning blue sky that poured in through the window. He stood from his chair, dragging it loudly on the stone floor, look-ing around out of habit rather than reason, and approached the object. Its vitreous surface now reflected his face back at him — a dark, distorted version of the king, with shadowed eyes and a blurry frown on his brow. He stared in bewilderment as he rubbed his long curly beard. The shadowy form did the same.

And there he stood, simply *looking* at his own dark reflection as the morning raced past. It was not until the door opened that he snapped out of his trance. "Petitioners, sire," his advisor said. The king looked back and quickly stepped away from the mysterious object, partly because he didn't want distractions from his now-pressing duties, and partly because he felt—for some obscure, petty, unconscious reason he could not explain—that he did not want to *share* this mystery.

It was a warm noon when the king came back from the banquet hall. Long was the day, and between dinner and his duties as monarch, he had not been able to return to his study, although he had made it explicit that no one should enter before him. He dropped his stack of parchment and letters and lightly jogged to the window, standing once more over the object, now reflecting his visage even more darkly, surrounded by the rubicund tones of dusk.

He wanted to touch it — oh, Lord, he really wanted to touch it, and why shouldn't he? He *was* king, after all — all in this island was his to touch; his intuition, which rarely failed, him assured him that it was safe; it was good. He reached out with his hand, trembling from some resurging teenage wanderlust, and lightly tapped the glossy black surface.

It lit up! *Magic*, he immediately thought; it had to be, for an emergent, flameless light shone from it like the moon. The strange letters now appearing on its surface were not any he could read or even recognize. He touched it again. The strange letters and symbols glided on its surface like boats on a bright, transparent sea, moving out of sight and deep back into wherever they had come from. Figures slowly emerged — they were people! The king sat down beside the object and cautiously lowered his head closer. The people quickly became bigger, encompassing the whole of the surface, making evident that which the king now realized: they were naked.

His lordship, chosen by God for His holy endeavor, was not adverse to nudity; he was married, after all, and many of the artworks that populated the island displayed the human form in all its natural glory. This, however, was different — the object projected on its surface the clear image of a woman and a man copulating, not sanctimoniously, not respectfully or in any manner of courtship, but primal. Their shapes were contorted like animals, fully given over to sinful carnal desires, their eyes steeped in lustful arrogance. He looked away.

How could he not? The king knew that he risked eternal damnation by simply looking, by simply acknowledging what he was looking at! This object was cursed—the work of the serpent, the great deceiver—he knew now with all certainty. The servants of the lord of lies are plentiful and crafty, that he knew, oh yes. Some must have infiltrated his palace — they must have come up from the rot and ruin and dirt of the city slums, oh yes! He had to call the guard, call the archbishop and rid himself of this now. He started towards the door... but he *paused.*

He paused, because behind his wall of sanctimonious purpose, a tree was growing. A twisting red tree that now dropped its phallic fruits all over and beyond the wall. The king was curious.

Without giving himself time to doubt or reconsider, the king doubled back and ran over to the object, instinctively touching the surface again, this time without care. And thus he knew his soul was captivated, because the once-still image was now moving, acting, just as if he had in front of himself a window into the sinful private life of the couple; the woman moaned, the man grunted, and the sounds of sex filled his study. He picked up the object. It was smooth, metallic, and very light. He moved it from side to side, up and down, but the image remained — this magical window, unshaken, ever true, focused on the action.

Fearing the commotion and unable to think straight, his head spinning, he touched the surface once more, directly on the woman's breasts as she rode the man. She froze, and so did he; the study fell silent as a grave. He could hear his heartbeat, the blood rushing behind his ears and the shuffling of his robe as he hid the object underneath.

Last days of autumn
"The holy king shits, and the people wipe."
— local expression

Months had passed since the fateful discovery, and unrest had grown in the streets of the capital. Bloody fights broke out often now, between the mainlanders and locals; the oldwives—always wise beyond their years—said violence was in the air, in the water, in the dirt.

The king, however, did not see much of this growing discontent. He solved as many disputes as he could when the petitions came, disputes that had turned from the economic to the physical. He conversed tentatively with the Church authority, requesting a drop in taxes for the Holy See. These were but half-measures; he knew it, and the nobility at the palace either quietly suspected or outright acknowledged it: for the first time in his life, the king was taking half-measures. His mind was preoccupied, silently overtaken by the need to explore his new magical artifact. He didn't shirk his duties, no, but they were becoming secondary — on some deep level of his psyche, the need to explore this cursed entity was rising in priority, and he used any justification possible to ignore the fact that he *knew* this was happening.

Temperatures had dropped significantly. The king lay covered in furs and blankets, door locked and cursed artifact in hand. He had made important discoveries in these few months of studies: first, the recorded intercourse would loop once finished, eternally bathing its surroundings in lustful depravity; second, the depravity was—as far as he could tell—endless, for if one were to drag his finger across the surface, one would not pause the act but exchange this window for another one. This way he had seen so many things he had not even thought of before — men and women of every shape and size, positions he couldn't even understand.

It was during what had now become his daily, routine round of scrolling that he found something captivating. It was a couple, like all the others, but the woman had a *terrifying* resemblance to his wife in her younger years. A surge of sadness and desire swept over him as he remembered what they had once been — what they had now lost. And the desire spread from his withering soul to his heart, and so his heartbeat quickened, and once more from his heart to his loins, stoking the fire. He reached under the blanket and got to work, sullying himself, sullying the holy sacred memory of his marriage and all the vows their god had placed as he pleasured himself, as this younger visage was sodomized.

He got to his bedchamber that night. His expression was

gloomy, and one could tell by his shambling that he had been emotionally exhausted. Like every night, he lay beside his wife in the dark and closed his weary eyes. The blanket of supple dreams had only begun to drop on him when it was taken back, ripped away as he opened his eyes again — his wife was talking to him.

"My love?" she whispered in the dark, "'tis a cold night, my love," she repeated as she cuddled him, her hand caressing his chest. As she traced circles over his heart, she spoke softly, her mature voice like sweet honey. "'Tis a cold night, but there, fire can be lit, and so we might... rid ourselves of this icy stiffness," she chuckled.

No answer.

"My love?" she prodded, her voice now accompanied by a hint of vulnerability. The king said nothing, turned away from her, and fell asleep.

Heart of winter
"If walkin' round, ye spot a rat
If the rodent be plump and fat
And our tongue it pitapat
Be sure to feed it to yer cat!"
— anti-mainlander nursery rhyme

Bitter wine tastes sweet because nothing is more sweet than the bitter hard work and time from which the flavor is derived. The royal advisor's wine was bitter, but for a long time now, it *tasted* bitter too. The king was absent; it was time to heed the petitioners, and he was absent once more, for the second time this month. And this was no minor dispute, no, no... it was murder

— a local bled dry by a mainlander after an insult turned into a fight, and then a battle. The other locals, family and friends, demanded reparations — demanded justice and severe action against the mainlander and his ilk. This was a widespread sentiment now. The royal advisor sighed; he would just have to take over as best he could to delay—yes, delay, not resolve—these disputes, until the king was... better equipped.

He had wondered, at first, if his liege was not perhaps sick. And so he had once, in the name of servitude and compliance with his duties, approached the king's study and had laid his ear upon the door. Moaning could be heard inside — a woman, passionately screaming in the height of ecstasy; the royal advisor had, at that moment, thought nothing of it and offered but a chuckle.

However, after this repeated itself multiple times, he began to wonder. When the queen confirmed, through painfully held-back tears, that she was not the one hollering in passion, he began to worry. Thus it went on; with each missed appointment, each rescheduled royal banquet, the unholy noises emanating from the king's study garnered an air of strangeness... Multiple female voices differing in intensity, multiple male voices, sometimes only men, sometimes only women. Sometimes from the king's study drifted a veritable cacophony of moans, slapping, and otherwise unsavory sounds orchestral in proportion. And the servants snickered and the staff whispered.

The royal advisor, whose wine now was always bitter, looked on with increasing worry as his king came out every morning slightly later, the dark, uneven contours ringing his eyes getting slightly bigger, his hair slightly messier.

First days of spring

— local revolutionary pamphlet

I cannot stop. These were the words that resonated within the king's scattered skull. He knew many things, as he always did. He knew the queen now despised him — he hadn't touched her in months. He knew rumors of his supposed sinful activities had spread like wildfire, and once they had consumed the palace, they had quickly flickered to every corner of the island and beyond. He knew this cursed artifact was destroying him; he was destroying himself, and, yet, *he couldn't stop.*

Every day, he would spend hours just scrolling and visualizing this deplorable medium, ransacking his senses and rotting his brain as his hand moved ever steadfastly. He shirked his duties, and he barely slept or ate. He could have anything he wanted; he was king, concubines and bastards were all too common, and his reach had been powerful and vast, craving every exotic taste. So why was he wasting his life away, look-

81

ing through this... *window*? What pushed him to give it all away for something that wasn't even really there? Was it for the sake of convenience? He wondered these things, in the lucid moments that he very rarely enjoyed. The king would wonder as he prayed in his room, hands on the cold stone floor, tears in his eyes: "Wickedness for the sake of wickedness! When that which is forbidden, dark, and sinful becomes routine, what happens to our souls, o Lord? Even now, my prayer is cut short, not for want but for need, an excuse so that my head I can lay in my chair again, and sell another piece of my mind, soul, and body to that infernal artifact!"

The royal advisor would bang on the door. Voice cracking, he would beg his liege for assistance, for clarity, for purpose, for him to go back to the man he once was. The man he could have always continued being. "O, my lecherous king!" he would supplicate, hands bleeding from the pounding at the door. "The revolutionaries have consorted with that horrid western king! He comes now, o lord of mine! With a hundred ships and a hundred more! And the streets hold their breath — it is all too close to chaos, to madness, but... but... you can still *fix* this, my lord! You can still make it right, prithee, come out!"

The banging continued, but the king could not hear. He was at the climax of the latest round of debauchery; this one had lasted for three hours, and he would need time to rest. Yes, only one more, and he would get to work.

Last days of spring

Partially recovered diary of King ——
The year of our lord ——
Last day of his rule

It is all over. I hear them — the revolutionaries and thieves and demons. They are raging outside, and soon they'll tear down the doors and take all that is mine. I don't care for my riches, they're all worthless anyway. I don't care for my wife. They can kill her, if it so pleases them, but they must never find my holy grail. I will hide it, hide it in the tunnels and chambers and deep where all light cannot reach, and if they find it, Lord above — I will destroy it before I share it. They're in the walls, there is screaming in the walls. They're coming. I think I have time for one more.

Patricide

They say that memories are what shape us, drive us, and, eventually, accompany us in our final instants before the voyage to the other side. Jan Torres had only good memories of his father; this, of course, was an exaggeration — there had been bad moments as with any human relationship, but he had admired no other, celebrated no other more than his father. And now the powerful torch that had once been Arlet Torres shone no brighter than a match, fizzling, its fickle flame slowly snuffed out by Alzheimer's.

And so Jan had slowly forgotten the bad times, locked them in a box and sent them deep within his unconscious mind, behind walls and doors of self, to be found and reopened again when the time was right — when *he* was ready.

For the last years of Arlet Torres' life, Jan would be the doting, hardworking son his father needed, even if Arlet didn't fully recognize that sometimes; even if Arlet didn't fully recognize *him* sometimes. But as old age crept up, it assisted those failings of the mind in extinguishing Arlet's already feeble light, until one day his life had to be transferred to the intensive care wing of the nearest hospital as per the new doctrine, his existence entombed within the sarcophagus of white walls, transparent tubing and stale sterilized air.

Jan would not be deterred, however; the hospital staff would take note, later telling of how devoted that son was, visiting room 153 every day. It was during one of these routine visits that Jan's world would collapse in on itself — for his father was awake that morning, sitting upright in his bed, nearly infinite gaze looking out the bright summer window, piercing through Jan as he turned around to look at his son, tears swelling in those perceptive, but fading, hazel eyes.

"I want to die." The words were soft; there was no hint of sarcasm in them, and their softness, a gesture to their unfortunate recipient, did not attempt to alleviate the severity of what they implied.

"I want to die," he repeated, more poignantly this time.

Jan's body and soul reeled as if impacted by a heavy object. He held back his tears and produced a wry, audibly fake laugh as he rushed to the bed and sat down beside his father, softly taking his hands and warmly caressing them, speaking slowly: "Papa, what's gotten into you? What do you mean you 'want to die' — does something hurt?"

His father shook his head, and Jan—under the impression that this was nothing more than another one of his lately common fugues—began to shift to the "call nurse" button near the bed. Arlet gripped his son's hands tighter, and Jan winced as he turned back, frustrated. "Papa! You're hurting me, what are you...?"

His hazel eyes were on him, that boundless gaze again. It was the feature that had always impressed Jan the most about his father — such intelligence behind that quiet look, such limitless potential, ideas and love, hidden but peeking through those brown orbs. It was him — that was Arlet Torres in his entirety, staring right at him, and Jan knew. He knew his father was here.

"Jan, my son," Arlet caressed his cheek. "I've been sleepy as of late, lost in thought and waking up confused, this morning I..." His voice choked with anguish, "I couldn't remember what your name was... my beautiful boy, the light of my life, the name your mother chose for you — God! How could I forget?!" Jan quickly hugged his father, unable to hold back a torrent of tears. It hurt to see him like this, hurt like nothing he had experienced before. Arlet, however, held back the tears, visibly wincing and struggling as he weathered the tide of emotion.

"I have thought about it..." he continued. "This isn't living, Jan, this is sinking, slowly into a pit that I can't escape from, a pit that will soon consume my thoughts and memories, the worst kind of prison! This is hell, and I want to die while still being... well... me! I want to die with the memories of the love of my life, and the perfect boy we made together..." He caressed Jan's curly hair, his old but expert touch rending Jan's heart even further, as thoughts of his childhood, all three of them together, clawed at his soul.

"I know how wrong, how horrible what I'm asking is. But, I... I have no one else," his voice quivered. Arlet knew the position he was putting his son in was hard, impossibly hard, both for his mind and for his future, but he was desperate; for the first time in his life, he was desperately pleading.

"I'm sorry, Jan," he repeated. "I..."

Suddenly, Jan's voice cut through the palpable emotion filling the room. "I will do it, Papa." Arlet's irises shone with renewed vigor, and they quivered with empowered sadness as the conflicting emotions overwhelmed him. His eyes watered, but he held strong, resolving to spend this moment of lucidity talking with his son.

They talked and talked until morning gave way to blazing hot summer midday. All manner of sentiments were shared. They talked of Jan's mother, of her dimples as she smiled, of her kindness as she cried. Jan hadn't realized just how much she adored him until late after her passing, *too late*.

They recounted—in that small, sterile room—a life lived together, with its ups and downs. But, ultimately, Arlet seemed satisfied, a contentedness engulfing his now placid brown eyes.

"It's time, Jan..." he announced, reclining and turning to look through the window at the bright streets below. "No-one else *really* visits me, and those that do... they wouldn't understand. Please, Jan," he begged. Jan was taken aback again — all of this talk about the past had pushed the responsibility and severity of the act deep down. His father's pleas were shunting it back up to the surface, and Jan shuddered — shuddered because he was not ready to do it now. Not now... he needed to think, plan it well, so he could have a life afterwards; he had to prepare himself, steel himself, to do the unthinkable.

"No, Papa!" Jan answered, stumbling over his words. "Don't you have anything else you want to do before... you know... and just like that? You can't just expect me to—"

"Do something else?" his father interjected, again offering a tragic, but contentedly warm, smile. "My beautiful boy... you allowed me to relive my entire life with the person that mattered most... with that still fresh in my mind, there is nothing else I want to do but finally rest,"

And so Jan was off, parting with a hug and a promise to return later that evening. "I love you," they had said to each other, and as he walked through the hospital doors he found the exchange to be out of place. Not because he didn't love his father — on the contrary, he had said that phrase so many times over the course of his life, to so many people, that it seemed too mundane for the occasion.

It was a large, rusty fan, hanging from the ceiling of the aged corner bar, that kept Jan's attention from the task at hand. He had decided, more on a whim than a thought, to plan his deed in a small local bar a few blocks from the hospital. And it was *local*, with its musty cigarette air, cacophony of loud conversations, the obtuse, barely functional fan giving it a strangely melancholic feel.

It made Jan feel like home, somehow, and with every loud spin of the fan's blades, so too spun his head around what he had to do, around what he felt. It spun around and around, making him sick to his stomach, making him furious; the bile within him taunted him with images he dared not even name.

"But this is what will allow my father to see himself," he told his sickening bile, and the sickening bile responded, "See himself for the last time, murderer..."

He ran to the bathroom and vomited. He needed to rid himself of the bile, some of it at least, for it did not only populate his stomach. He stood in the bathroom, washing his face with the old faucet under the bathroom mirror, washing the bad taste out, and letting his mind fly.

He would need to make it as painless as possible, that much was obvious. To Jan's bereft benefit, in a twist of fetid irony, the very same government whose policies forbade him from the act also assisted him — that same government was too poor to afford security cameras in every care room in the country. Many methods ran through his head, leaving their own pinpricks of emotional pain behind, feeding the bile that now rushed to his

cranium, to his face. Bubble in the IV? No, too unpredictable...
poison? No, too obvious... Smothering...?

He looked into the dirty mirror and saw a stranger looking
back. Who was this murderer coldly gazing through the glass?
Who was this monster that now thought to venture to the hospital to smother his own father? He didn't want his father to keep
on living just for his sake. For his sake, he wanted him to keep
on living. His anger rose once again, two waves of conflicting
emotions clashing within him, a cascade of pain spilling out of
his eyes in two waterfalls.

Through it all, his reflection didn't cry; it simply stared with
dead eyes, a black soul, a warning. It warned of a soundless
scream and a broken heart. He looked down and hit himself
in the head a few times, a childhood neuroticism long since forgotten, punching his cranium until the searing headache and
disorientation beckoned him to stop. Again he looked up, wincing and still crying, and through the mirror Jan stared back with
reddened eyes. There was no dark reflection; it had always been
just him. He left the bar in a hurry and made his way to the
hospital.

The nurses would comment on Jan's appearance that night,
on how the man walked resolutely to the intensive care wing of
the hospital. They would comment that nothing was different
from any other of his visits. It was only the janitor who had a
thought that would never be told to anyone.

The young man walked past the janitor. He hid it well, but his
steps were heavy, and for a fraction of a second the janitor saw
it: the boy was covered in chains. Heavy chains, slowly formed
from the dust of his sadness; this was grief, on an incomprehen-

sible level. The chains slowed him down and choked him.

Jan stood in front of the blank door, beside the sign reading *153*. The door handle rattled, more than it should have. Jan's hand shook uncontrollably. He walked into the dimly-lit room. Shuffling sounds came from the nearby bed as the timid voice of Arlet Torres cautiously pierced the dark, aimed vaguely at the intruding figure.

"Who's there?"

Jan stood there as his eyes began to water. His breath was caught up in his throat and all that came out at first was an anguished croak. His father looked on in horror. "It's me, Papa, don't you see? It's Jan..."

"Who are you? I don't know who Jan is, but I've got a wonderful son... my boy, he... he comes here every day to take care of me. He's such a good boy..."

Jan lifted a nearby pillow off of the couch and steadily approached. Arlet cowered on the bed like a frightened mouse, begging, "Please... I don't know what I've done to you, but... please let me call my son, he's such a kind boy, he'll get everything sorted out... please... I don't want to die..."

Jan opened his mouth to scream, but no sound came out. His hand, already balled up into a fist, now beckoned him to smash his own brain in. He had to, otherwise the chattering sound of his soul breaking would drive him mad. He stood there, mouth agape, straining, crying, and hitting himself in the head over and over again.

Though I be not your factor friend,
by prime exponent I ascend.
Each subtle facet that you see
uncovers a piece of mystery.
So gather my building blocks in turn —
from silent powers, the truth you'll learn.
Only then shall all be shown,
the hidden story that I own.

I AM ANNINGAN, BUT 2582249878086908589655919172004590033183495956083645630886764615976763811893327171511493895442004631241699602224973600768722811218966622081497356731130243011379494446786351592706821211974184745473764439126666851047072343635238064111457142999351076044591957074701853228891145592801684263052957280735306758435178528434798650753778146137760581442670803746385329456003262799068971565721378730756661470044733554626437444859145998588683330732201086893730863502714494955065814371486546817326756344875842243471764181558240513048890439514777508445340031517761092516591748919408271469955519965748329461126225620950852666696924663542446592917703648909599507744042980087204253429251214686757057298925979357877916829156721185349639573890773445440581016892616854841913054930552374902055268720382421247216659775709607305203140393145375760416322276046886499691633838371269510884703455866950315191566637570983858263262810916652107743467865700846454993412145907336673946356299096923271456685475549856393894402262725500102975925310547005768403062654731166098593531440949

9710508486680779599636840919525834439394131061729727

011135056556333527551789028291686678707106594155444355

569447021759658652060557684334551117499023806293516665

319279048254528696686890618223377226662219937308987

358724533712818626335280383977908681721103111422465026

922634171514524160651587678701594777798992166051364605

520596077525656893799207697264672694639506282636781483

094284272443262224742238338304800724588288780319944

767063821230369472529149288977937243221216691202493

654090846435408515298471372065663766430917277817911424

987072994661358126669292373072624707063189650856455030

865099233543475515741340736697943544691968079933379

698508478947547952824583326237758336875612824727370850

08498862496156476578377419872197228802802250048587573

837387016737129459764913779158530794406753706639208172

215736670585816773779949297466653818602863393823262143

833122494005373639224686279124820680214645934447019

9055559338520736176387032455417341305905515803970416

876398351831898984160586781686090415537443005214342416

425122685311311149601618687467572355185360714360738282

375958192139648400607647435662775469435293396728319144

258944730626430538947388289909242337798415248933820

269653055523623521640434342325156357899791680953423

219444247054079562993001012240540763725507207892717

705552285241532995547096043570115162571173070484458062

512942321249350558758638089806673534479225271156562

917968009089468120719512525260951367704701866357528145

573857044693809322428483743346072959102133869067276

839224669179712458682512097065868619229353775309183258

6254631319889378339635034357948247066694984959640538
3273615608829339914263796051792295326143011305863 84871
48715223055236482164909284015473355911735275602756 1712
19076439885635691292595975624737966041725247109933042
23159647427720081266358969055434014229841055971698249
34001529776362047129030198921142253217583979397056 7635
96313043735441483934665557027778108345086530714517 27487
07568990770883806500470454376141426624601857284610230
59384738999658003331913843046261011971512196340283 8573
25523669665239477446637933800889497912051077143254383
38861222511827950227113656039696229894931527058464849
68092324620695047603473101186152877210804111771255 9095
93531921974222137807394289268847469958251404844060 79
75614143934193630226997362503669980279328596741741 7445
32002628185352900130516229362301334060107720832171469
88303968789738221050280022600576476517759228196118574
71364464054473200195268336114284956126344328969575 2718
62769081985024303806182110727900076330784269198105 164
53716308335649864140894074020302519122337689938145691
51762667365965932022606444196644140183882925684920833
91394338638443613513850920293114217820650779187065 1901
83756079997739729174971038200870572782531772500952435
25177265419673058177731878336794167521925790732943 13192
10603223784865269939367851903995907703943010655 1936
70264959863968438787295689623701464182603705349973728
08652569343400124917308145521931587675799443264524 9781
50449973407941589577917495864901955233901188367252 8369
73246007683795459601280657500254747440186359446445 60
766078647555632015235125888314263232319033703213043146

88947575414393672924139454507759654842230051563958454 6
57570836724379013346033926206655880375023959792863 76
63965127512232369148099370950336577743517417640486457 0
74160651306813471048562987133640046996399314230711809
49008807170254322161613980238433077915240082034684840
33215600495630024436013228263729753319301865218335312
18530114414085396375154491396356405186924061113769038 78
38348415053952015252071618148146929926465060051677551 2
59975000545361481709003786290440912413945102271496104
59911720878715178668282374159704031862576454463762862 52
49419521178757129543814907163944386096076575825330049 9
86512627241512559570778373452666113217337549794813074747
61552186591129746324669173622687766787542066863094445 5
28057767358465434271546581229729666501364491241471205 71
58479276599520360932560763986008501049521204597719 80
05733388180019568526630381297891847022991441127740306 5
91328646057860993085668148960237427627271270697248643
67126411664450797868691570741283464470649296078708722 0
85152516593415510545457952749204171279432549255529137467
53526098824404046751917629820607720666130298400059 0
96627839473402265741206062336941637227622402376559879
36251668268952509214222696531547923195120953696209348
26428323909682997490731160751136199494259593332198743
2501

...to all those who support this still-cursed man —
I will forever repay you with my own.

www.ingramcontent.com/pod-product-compliance
Lightning Source LLC
LaVergne TN
LVHW090116180726
843489LV00002B/852